D0996017

SHEEP AT THE SHOW

They scrambled up the wall and down the other side. There were two men, darting around, flapping their hands and shouting at the sheep. One of the men was Mr Ingrams, the gliding club manager. He looked up and saw Mandy, James and Harriet.

'Do something quickly!' he yelled urgently, pointing skywards. 'Look!'

'Cripes! There's a glider. It must be coming in to land!' gasped James.

Harriet took control. She rattled out instructions and Mandy and James moved in the direction she told them to.

The three of them had just got the sheep bunched together when Mr Ingrams and one of the other men shot towards them, yelling frantically.

They looked behind. The glider was coming right at them . . .

Animal Ark series

LUCY DANIELS

Sheep

— *at the* —

Show

Illustrations by Jenny Gregory

Hodder
Children's
Books

a division of Hodder Headline plc

Special thanks to Pat Posner
Thanks also to C. J. Hall, B.Vet.Med., M.R.C.V.S., for reviewing
the veterinary material contained in this book.

Text copyright © 1998 Ben M. Baglio
Created by Ben M. Baglio, London W12 7QY
Illustrations copyright © 1998 Jenny Gregory

First published in Great Britain in 1998
by Hodder Children's Books

The right of Lucy Daniels to be identified as the Author of this Work
has been asserted by her in accordance with the Copyright, Designs
and Patents Act 1988.

10 9 8 7 6 5 4 3 2 1

All rights reserved. No part of this publication may be reproduced,
stored in a retrieval system, or transmitted, in any form or by any
means without the prior written permission of the publisher, nor be
otherwise circulated in any form of binding or cover other than that
in which it is published and without a similar condition being
imposed on the subsequent purchaser.

All characters in this publication are fictitious and any resemblance
to real persons, living or dead, is purely coincidental.

A Catalogue record for this book is available from the British Library

ISBN 0 340 69950 7

Typeset by Avon Dataset Ltd, Bidford-on-Avon, Warks

Printed and bound in Great Britain by
Clays Ltd, St Ives plc

Hodder Children's Books
a division of Hodder Headline plc
338 Euston Road
London NW1 3BH

One

'Mandy!' called Emily Hope from the foot of the stairs. 'You'll be late if you don't get a move on.'

'Just coming, Mum!' Mandy called back, ramming a couple more things into her backpack. It was the day before half-term holiday at Walton Moor School, and Mandy was going on a school trip to the new gliding club near Upper Syke Moor.

The club had a field centre and the pupils from Classes 7 and 8 were visiting it as part of a technology and design project to make their own model glider. They'd be learning about the sort of weather needed for gliding, measuring up a glider and making sketches of it. Then, after their half-term break, they'd start to draw up their own plans at school.

But more exciting, Mandy thought as she dashed downstairs, would be the gliding display the club manager had arranged. It was taking place after lunch. Mandy was looking forward to that most of all, and she knew her best friend, James Hunter, and most of their classmates were too.

'It's OK, you can slow down,' said Mr Hope as Mandy burst into the kitchen. 'I promised the Spry sisters I'd call in sometime this morning to give Patch his cat flu injection. You can put your bike in the back of the Land-rover and I'll run you to school first, Mandy. I'll go to The Riddings on my way back.'

'Thanks, Dad,' said Mandy. 'But could we pick up James, please? He'll be waiting at the crossroads for me.'

'No problem,' said her dad, getting to his feet.

A few minutes later they were ready to leave. Mandy turned in her seat to look at her mum who was standing by the front door of the old stone cottage, under the wooden sign that said 'Animal Ark, Veterinary Surgery'.

Both Mandy's parents were vets and it always amused her that the cottage as well as their surgery

– a modern extension built on at the back – was called Animal Ark. ''Bye!' she called, waving through the open window.

'Have a good time,' called Emily Hope, waving back.

James was already at the Fox and Goose crossroads. His head swung round as he heard the Land-rover, then he grinned as it drew up beside him. Mandy jumped down to open the back and help him put his bike in.

'There's no breeze at all today,' he pointed out gloomily, after he'd climbed in and said hello to Mr Hope. 'I bet the gliders won't be able to go up.'

'I shouldn't worry, James,' said Mr Hope. 'It's usually windier up on the moors.'

They were soon out of the village and driving up the hilly moorland road that led to Walton, the town nearest to Welford.

As they drove past the end of a narrow lane that wound its way up to the higher moorland, Mandy noticed someone in the distance cycling slowly up it.

'I thought for a minute that was Harriet,' she said to James.

'The new girl who started school yesterday?'

Mandy nodded and looked puzzled. 'It couldn't have been her, though. She was going the wrong way.'

'Maybe she decided to go back home,' suggested James. 'When I saw her at break she didn't seem to want to make friends with anyone. And she wasn't exactly enthusiastic about coming on the trip when Susan Collins came round asking for names.'

Harriet was in Mandy's class but Mandy had spent all her free time the day before helping Miss Hooper, one of the teachers who were taking them on the field trip, print out timetables and worksheets. She hadn't had any time to talk to the girl with the mop of short black curly hair, dark brooding eyes and sulky-looking mouth.

'It must be hard starting a new school halfway through a term,' said Mandy. Then she forgot about the new girl as she looked out of the window at the scenery. The rough moorland pastures, separated by grey drystone walls, stretched up to the flanks of the impressive purple fells rolling across the skyline.

'There's Upper Syke Moor.' Mandy pointed to a moor rising up way over to their right. It looked lovely in early summer with the purple heather in bloom and the sheep scattered over it.

James nodded. 'The gliding club is on the big plateau below Upper Syke Moor. I can't wait to get there,' he added. 'It should be fun.'

'I thought you were going there to learn something, not to have fun,' teased Mr Hope.

'Mr Haynes and Miss Hooper are in charge,' Mandy told him. 'They'll make sure we learn a lot. They're both really strict.'

'They're OK, though,' said James. 'They suggested the trip when we heard there was a field centre attached to the gliding club.'

'I think having the field centre there was the thing that enabled Sam Western to get planning permission for the gliding club,' said Mr Hope. 'Dora Janeki and a couple of other sheep farmers with grazing rights on Upper Syke Moor protested about it. They thought the gliders might worry the sheep.'

'Sam Western nearly always gets his own way,' said Mandy. She didn't like the wealthy landowner and dairy farmer at all. He and his farm manager had once tried to poison Houdini – a gorgeous goat belonging to a friend of theirs, Lydia Fawcett.

'He didn't get his own way about the disused quarry that's on some of his land,' said James. 'He was supposed to have it filled in last year but he didn't bother getting it done. Someone told my mum that the new people at Quarry Cottage complained about it to the safety officer at the Town Hall. Now, Mr Western's been told he's got a month to get it filled in or he'll be in big trouble.'

'Knowing him, he'll still find a way round it,' said Mandy.

When Mr Hope drew up outside the school there was already a small group waiting by the gates. Most of them knew Mandy's dad and called a greeting to him as he got out to open the back of the Land-rover for Mandy and James.

'Thanks for the lift, Mr Hope,' said James, as he got his bike out.

Mandy reached up to kiss her dad goodbye.

'Have a good time,' he said, giving her a lop-sided smile before getting back into the Land-rover.

'I'll take our bikes to the bike shed,' offered James. 'You join the queue for the coach so we can get a good seat.'

It wasn't long before the coach appeared. Everyone cheered. Then Mr Haynes and Miss Hooper arrived to read out names and check that everyone was present.

But there was no answer to one of the names in

Mandy's class. Harriet Ruck, the new girl, wasn't there.

'Has anyone seen her?' Miss Hooper asked with a frown.

Mandy wondered if she ought to tell the teacher that she thought she had seen Harriet cycling in the wrong direction. But she decided not to. She didn't want to get Harriet into trouble.

'Harriet did say she was coming, didn't she?' said Miss Hooper, after she'd called out the rest of the names. 'Who wrote this list?'

'I did, Miss Hooper,' said Susan Collins. 'Harriet did bring a permission slip back, so I put her name down. Perhaps she's sick.'

There was still no sign of Harriet by the time Mr Haynes had stowed all the backpacks into the luggage compartment. Miss Hooper said they'd have to go without her. 'And I'll have to go to the secretary's office and ask her to phone Mrs Ruck to confirm that Harriet isn't with us,' she added. 'You can get on the bus while I'm doing that. And settle yourselves down quickly. We've wasted enough time as it is.'

'I'll tell that new girl a thing or two when I see her,' muttered Becky Severn. 'If Miss Hooper's in a bad mood it's Harriet's fault.'

But when Miss Hooper returned and slipped into her seat, she reminded them with a smile to keep the noise down so the driver could concentrate.

And, half an hour later, they were turning off the moorland road that James and Mandy travelled every day and on to the unmade road that led to the gliding club.

It was a narrow, twisty lane. Mandy wondered what would happen if they were to meet someone coming away from the club, towing a glider or a trailer.

'I expect the club members have to use the road from the other side of the moor,' James told her. 'It's much wider than this one. *And* smoother,' he added as they went over a bump.

After ten minutes of jolts and bumps, the coach came to a halt in the club's carpark.

'Is this it?' Justin Simpson stared through the window. 'I thought we'd come to see gliders, not a massive, empty field.'

'They're probably all f lying!' said Vicki, his twin, pushing past a couple of the other children to peer upwards through one of the windows.

'If you two had taken the trouble to look at the timetable and worksheet I gave you yesterday afternoon, you'd know the sequence of events,' Miss

Hooper told them crisply. 'The gliders won't be arriving here until this afternoon,' she informed them.

When they got off the coach, Mr Haynes told them to stand still and quietly while he handed out their backpacks.

But suddenly, Justin Simpson pointed to the car-park entrance and gave a low whistle. The others turned their heads to see Harriet Ruck cycling towards them. Miss Hooper didn't have to tell them to stay where they were; one icy look was enough to make them stand and wait while she strode over to Harriet.

After a short conversation, Miss Hooper wheeled Harriet's bike over to the coach and put it inside. Harriet followed, dragging her feet and looking embarrassed.

Mr Haynes didn't give anyone time to ask questions. 'The gliding club manager will be waiting in the clubhouse for us,' he said. 'So let's get a move on, please.'

The club's manager, Josh Ingrams, welcomed them with a friendly smile. 'I don't know if any of you remember this building before it was renovated and turned into our clubhouse,' he said. 'It used to be a shieling, a place where a shepherd tended any sick sheep he'd brought down off the moor.'

He went on to explain that, although it had been derelict for years, the sheep had been in the habit of coming down from the moor and using the building as a shelter. 'So, before we started renovating it, and marking out the landing area, we had to rebuild all the drystone walls and put wire fencing in place to keep them out of the field.'

James looked at Mandy and smiled when Mr Ingrams added, 'Still, you haven't come to hear or think about animals.' James knew she was enjoying Mr Ingrams's little speech.

After that, Mr Ingrams led them to the building that had been added on for the field centre where one of the club's gliding instructors would be giving the weather talk.

He opened a door leading off from the clubhouse into an airy room. The tables, chairs, large whiteboard and easel made it look like a classroom. Under the big plate-glass windows that overlooked the take-off and landing field, there was a row of binoculars mounted on tripods.

Mandy, James and a few others ran over to use the binoculars.

'Wow, they're powerful!' said Mandy. 'They make

the sheep on the moor look like they're just the other side of the window.'

The one wall that didn't have any windows was covered in photographs and posters and plans of gliders with names like *Swift, Swallow, Skylark, Molly Hawk* and *Buzzard*.

'You'll be seeing quite a few gliders with birds' names today,' said Mr Ingrams.

'But will we see them in the air?' asked James. He was still worrying about the weather.

Mr Ingrams said the pilots were putting on a display at another club that morning, then coming straight back. 'By air,' he added with a smile.

'So we'll be able to watch them arriving!' said James. 'That'll be brilliant.'

'First things first,' said Miss Hooper. 'Come and sit down, please.'

Harriet hung back until everyone else was seated then she went and sat at a table on her own. A few of them gave her curious looks but she just stared straight ahead. Becky Severn caught Mandy's eye and put a finger under her nose – miming that Harriet was stand-offish.

Mandy shrugged. The new girl certainly seemed to want to keep herself to herself.

After the talk and a short break it was time to go

into the hangar and measure up the *Kirby Kite* – the glider they'd be copying for their model.

Measuring the glider took them quite a long time. But at last they'd all taken every measurement they thought they'd need and it was time for lunch in the clubhouse.

Suddenly, over the excited chatter, came the sound of sheep baa-ing.

'The farmers must be bringing them down off the moor,' said Mandy. 'It's about time for shearing, so they're probably rounding them up to take them back to the farms.'

Lunch was just about over when Josh Ingrams appeared, looking worried. 'We've got a problem,' he announced. 'The sheep have managed to find a way into the field. They're all over the place.'

Chairs scraped and voices rose as everyone made to dash to the door.

'Back to your seats, please!' Mr Haynes ordered. 'Looking at the sheep won't solve the problem.'

'We need a sheepdog to do that,' said Mr Ingrams. 'I've tried phoning the farmers who own the wretched animals but neither of them is in. If we don't get the sheep out the gliders won't be able to land!'

Mandy and James glanced at each other. Perhaps there was another solution.

Two

'James and I could probably drive the sheep out, Miss Hooper,' offered Mandy. 'We've watched sheepdogs rounding up sheep lots of times.'

'We've helped out with lambing on a sheep farm as well,' said James.

Mandy and James waited impatiently while Mr Ingrams and the two teachers discussed it.

'Very well, Mandy,' Miss Hooper said. 'You and James go and see what you can do.'

'I'll just get some binoculars, then I'll come with you to see if I can spot how they got in,' said Mr Ingrams.

'Cripes!' said James when they went outside.

'They really *are* all over the place, aren't they?' In every direction he looked he saw sheep. The lambs – almost as big as the ewes now – were bleating loudly as they darted around trying to find their own mum.

'There! Look!' said Mandy, pointing down to the very far end of the field. 'There are two more coming over the wall right now.'

Mr Ingrams raised the binoculars to his eyes. 'Part of the wall's down. That's how they got in all right.'

'It's a shame they didn't flock together in that far corner,' said James. 'It would've been easy to get them back to the broken-down bit then.'

'Mmm,' Mandy nodded. Her eyes were on the sheep as she tried to work out the best way of driving them back down to the end of the field. Most of them seemed to be making for the landing area. The grass was a darker green there; perhaps it looked more appetising.

'How about taking a gentle run at the others to get them on to the landing area too?' James suggested.

'Good idea,' Mandy agreed. 'Let's walk slowly down the field at first, then split and speed up. You go to the left and I'll go to the right.'

'OK,' said James. 'And once we've got them in more of a bunch, with any luck we'll only need to clap and shout a bit to get a few moving off in the right direction.'

Mandy nodded. 'With a bit more luck, the rest will probably follow.'

'I'll go and phone Wotton Gliding Club,' Mr Ingrams told them. 'I might just be in time to get them to delay take off for an hour.'

'I hope it doesn't take us an hour to get them out!' said James as he and Mandy started walking down the field.

'It might,' said Mandy. 'There's an awful lot of them, James.'

As they approached the sheep Mandy said, 'OK, James. Split!'

Mandy set off at a slow run to the right, taking a wide circle behind the straggling sheep. Then, approaching three or four sheep grazing quite close together from the side, she made shooting movements with her hands. To her delight they began to run towards the landing area.

She used the same tactics on another small group but the sheep split up and ran in different directions. Trying to remember how sheepdogs worked, Mandy ran, slowed, circled and stood.

She began to feel worried. If she and James couldn't get the sheep out, the gliders wouldn't be able to land. The whole day would be ruined. Mandy wondered how James was doing across at the other side, but she didn't dare take her eyes off the sheep. And now this second group finally seemed to have made up their minds all to go in one direction.

'The wrong direction though,' Mandy murmured as she moved quickly to the front of them. She waved her arms and they turned. They, too, made their way towards the landing area.

Mandy heaved a sigh of relief as the sheep stood bunched together. But her sigh turned to one of despair as two sheep at the front of the bunch suddenly moved away. Before she had time to think what to do, the rest of the bunch followed in an untidy, straggly line.

Mandy glanced over towards James. He was flapping his arms wildly at his lot of sheep as he ran. His method seemed to be working well until the sheep who'd broken away from Mandy met them and the whole lot scattered in different directions.

Mandy heard pounding feet and looked over her shoulder to see who was coming. To her amazement it was Harriet Ruck.

'You're going the wrong way about it,' said Harriet. 'You should both be working on opposite sides but working *together* to get all the sheep bunched at the same time. You have to watch each other as well as watching the sheep.

'I'll work with you, and *you* . . .' Harriet glanced at James, '. . . you go back over to the left of that lot and drive them towards us. Remember, keep your eyes on us as well as on the sheep.'

Mandy soon realised that Harriet knew exactly what she was doing. Every now and then, as they darted back and forth, she tersely reminded Mandy to check James, or called to James to look at what she and Mandy were doing. And all the time the sheep were gradually forming themselves into a bunch *and* they were all facing in the same direction.

'OK!' Harriet called at last. 'Get behind them now and run them towards the wall. I'll sort any who try to break away.'

Eventually, the first few sheep at the front were scrabbling their way back over the broken wall. Breathing hard, Mandy, James and Harriet stood watching them. Then the rest of the sheep started following quickly.

Mandy glanced at Harriet, wanting to say 'well

done', but Harriet's face was all closed up and she kept her eyes on the sheep.

'Some are marked with a blue J,' Mandy said. 'They must be Dora Janeki's.'

James managed a weak grin. 'And your dad said she thought the gliders might worry the sheep. If her sheep do this too often it'll be the other way round. Uh-oh!' he added, pointing. 'We've got two breakaways!'

'One's a different breed,' said Mandy. 'Can you see, James? It's got a longer coat and brown markings. And look at those lovely curly horns!'

'It's smaller than the others,' said James, sprinting off to try and get behind it.

The second breakaway sheep stopped suddenly. It seemed to be watching the brown-and-white one, which had turned again now, and was going back towards James.

James dashed sideways then tried to circle it. The sheep started running in circles too. James clapped his hands and shouted. The second sheep bleated loudly and moved towards the circling one who was moving faster and faster. It suddenly started running in a straight line. It was heading for the stone wall, but not the broken-down part.

To Mandy's amazement the sheep didn't slow

down; it just kept running. It ran straight into the wall! Mandy winced as she heard the thump. Then the sheep backed away, shaking its head.

'James!' gasped Mandy. 'That must have hurt her! Should we try to do something?'

'But what can we do?' asked James, looking worried.

'I'm not sure.' Mandy nibbled her lip thoughtfully. 'Harriet, can you think of anything?'

Harriet didn't answer. She stood as still as a statue, her face stony, her eyes fixed on the brown-and-white sheep, her lips folded tight in a straight line.

'Look!' James whispered. 'That other sheep is moving towards her. It's banging against her. Mandy! Is it going to attack her or something?'

Mandy felt her whole body tense. She was just about to throw herself forward when Harriet flung out an arm to prevent her. 'Can't you see that the Jacob is blind and the other sheep is helping her?' she said in a harsh whisper. 'If you interfere you'll panic the blind one and then she might really hurt herself. Just keep still and watch.'

Mandy blinked. Harriet hadn't raised her voice above that strange harsh whisper but it was clear she was either very annoyed or very upset. But there was no time to think.

The two sheep were now moving slowly – the second one staying slightly behind. Every now and then, when the brown-and-white sheep hesitated or wavered, the bigger one nudged it. It was guiding her along, making her walk towards the broken-down bit of wall.

Mandy wondered what would happen when the two sheep reached the broken portion. Perhaps she and James should sneak along behind them, so they could push them through the gap. She was about to suggest this when James grabbed her arm.

'Look! The big one's pushing hard against the brown-and-white one,' he said. 'That must be to make her turn. Yes, yes, it is.'

The brown-and-white sheep stood still, facing the broken-down wall. The bigger one moved to her back end and, with an urgent-sounding bleat, gave her a firm nudge, encouraging her to go through the gap. Then she moved quickly to the right and pushed hard against the other sheep's flank.

'She's helping her get over the lowest bit,' said Mandy.

A couple of seconds later, the brown-and-white

sheep had made it safely to the other side of the wall.

Mandy turned to look at James, her eyes shining. 'I'd never have believed this if we hadn't seen it happening!'

'She's not going the same way as the others, though,' James pointed out.

'Maybe she doesn't belong with them,' said Mandy. 'Dad said something about other farmers with grazing rights on the moor, remember?'

'There goes her helper,' said James, 'running to get in front of her.'

'She's banging her shoulder to make her turn round,' said Mandy.

The brown-and-white sheep bleated softly as she turned, and her companion bleated back. Then, side by side, they made their way to join the rest of the flock.

James took off his glasses and polished them with his T-shirt. 'Amazing!' he said quietly.

Mandy nodded and looked at Harriet again. Mandy was almost sure there were tears in the other girl's dark brown eyes. But then they heard voices and running footsteps, and Harriet turned away.

'We're going to build the wall back up!' yelled Justin Simpson. 'Mr Ingrams says the gliders will be here in about twenty minutes.'

'We were all watching you,' panted Vicki. 'You made brilliant sheepdogs once Harriet came and showed you how!'

'Yes. Well done,' said Miss Hooper.

'Could I go and phone Animal Ark, Miss Hooper?' Mandy asked. 'The brown-and-white sheep couldn't see where it was going. It might need treatment and Mum or Dad might know who owns it. I'm sure it shouldn't be with the others. It could hurt itself up on the moor.'

'All right,' Miss Hooper nodded.

Harriet glared hard at Mandy. Then she walked over and picked up one of the stones from the wall and staggered over to Mr Ingrams with it.

As she and James raced back to the clubhouse, Mandy wondered why Harriet had looked at her like that. But she didn't wonder for long. At the moment her main concern was for the beautiful brown-and-white sheep.

'Dad says the sheep sounds like a Jacob. That's what Harriet said it was, isn't it?' said Mandy, joining James after she'd phoned Animal Ark. 'But he doesn't know anyone with a Jacob sheep so he's going to phone Dora Janeki and ask her about it.'

'What did he say when you told him the sheep couldn't see?' asked James, handing Mandy an ice-cold can of Coke.

'He said there's a sort of virus that affects sheeps' eyes and makes them temporarily blind,' Mandy replied. 'If that's what's wrong with the poor sheep, it needs treatment.'

Just then the gliding instructor who'd given the weather talk walked over to them. 'Well done,' he said. 'I wouldn't have had a clue about shifting that lot.'

'We weren't doing too well until Harriet came,' Mandy told him.

'Well, thank heavens you got them out, anyway. There could have been a very nasty accident if the glider pilots had been forced to make an emergency landing on the moors.'

'Look!' shouted James. 'Gliders!'

'And here come Miss Hooper and the others,' said Mandy. 'What great timing!'

'Mmm,' murmured James, his eyes skywards.

The gliding instructor gave a running commentary as the gliders landed, then led them all over to the landing strip.

After they'd looked at the gliders and talked to the pilots, there was a surprise announcement.

Instead of an ordinary display, the gliders were going to have a race.

'Race?' Susan Collins gasped, looking excited.

'Yup.' One of the pilots nodded and pointed. 'Six of us will race along the front edge of that flatter hill over there, from one end to the other,' he said. 'And,' he added, with a knowledgeable look at the sky, 'I reckon conditions are almost perfect right now.'

A few minutes later the pilots who were taking part in the race began pushing their gliders towards the winch launch that used a powerful engine on the ground to provide the power needed for launching.

Mandy, James and the other children raced over to where Mr Haynes and Miss Hooper were waiting to hand out binoculars.

They watched as the long cable, attached to the winch at one end, was connected to the first glider's release hook.

'Look, Mandy,' said James. 'The pilot's signalling to the winch operator. That must mean he's ready!'

They saw the slack in the cable taken up, then the cable being pulled fast enough to give the glider flying speed. Everyone let out a cheer as it took off.

The gliding instructor told them the pilot would release the cable when the glider reached maximum height. 'Then,' he said, 'the free end is retrieved and taken to the next glider to be launched.'

When the rest of the gliders were in the air, the race began. Everyone started shouting for the one they wanted to win. 'C'mon, *Ridge Rat!*' shouted Justin, trying to drown out his twin sister's voice as she yelled for her favourite.

Mandy shouted for *Sundancer*. The gliders were flying at different heights. For a while it was hard to tell which one was in the lead.

But *Sundancer* was lagging well behind and Mandy groaned with disappointment. She noticed James's choice, *Buzzard*, a glider with the wings going forward, seemed to be doing well. But, in the end, *Molly Hawk* was declared the winner.

'That's it, folks,' said the gliding instructor.

Mr Haynes glanced at his watch. 'Hand in your binoculars and then you can have ten minutes to relax and cool down before we get ready to go,' he told them.

Now the excitement was over, Mandy began to worry about the brown-and-white sheep again; and she also had time to wonder about the new girl.

How was it she'd seemed to know so much about rounding-up sheep, and that the brown-and-white one was a Jacob?

'It is strange,' James agreed, when Mandy told him what she'd been thinking. 'Shall we go and ask her?'

'We might get our heads bitten off, but we can try,' Mandy replied with a grin. 'Where is she? I can't see her. Can you, James?'

They wandered around but there was no sign of Harriet. None of the others seemed to know where she was, either.

'She isn't in the washroom,' said Susan Collins. 'I've just come from there.'

'Maybe she's waiting on the coach,' said Becky. 'We'll soon find out,' she added as Mr Haynes called out, telling them to fetch their backpacks and then make their way to the coach.

But Harriet wasn't there and neither was her bike! She'd obviously left and gone home on her own.

The new girl was certainly a bit of a mystery. Mandy met James's eyes. 'We'll work on it,' she said. 'But more important, I hope Dad's managed to find out who owns the Jacob.'

'Dora Janeki is sure to know,' James replied. 'I

bet everything will be sorted out by the time we get home.'

Mandy nodded. 'If it isn't, we'll have to do something about it ourselves,' she said determinedly.

Three

'I've got to bring Blackie to Animal Ark for his booster injection tomorrow morning,' said James, as he and Mandy slowed their bikes at the crossroads. 'But will you phone me if there's any news about the Jacob?'

'Of course I will,' Mandy replied. Then she was off, her blonde hair flying out as she pedalled towards Animal Ark.

There was no sign or sound of anyone when she opened the kitchen door and went in. She put her backpack on the table then went through to the surgery. The door to the treatment room opened and Mr Hope looked out.

'Mandy! I've just finished cleaning up. Did you have a good time?'

'Fantastic,' Mandy replied. 'There was a brilliant race along the edge of the moor. What's been happening here, Dad? Did you find out anything about the Jacob?'

'I'm afraid not, love. I've tried phoning Dora Janeki a few times, but she must be busy with the sheep. I managed to get hold of a couple of other farmers with grazing rights on the moor and they don't know anyone who owns a Jacob. They didn't seem too pleased to hear there was a foreigner amongst their sheep, especially one who might have an infection!'

Mandy sighed and looked worried.

'I'll try Dora again first thing in the morning,' said Mr Hope. 'That'll probably be the best time to catch her in.'

'Or James and I could go up to Syke Farm,' Mandy said. She tried to conceal a huge yawn.

Mr Hope smiled. 'I think you need an early night,' he said.

'I think you're right,' Mandy agreed. 'It was tiring work rounding up those sheep. Where's Mum?'

'It's her yoga night,' Adam Hope reminded her.

Mandy nodded. 'And are there any newcomers in the residential unit?'

'Just Flo Maynard's Butch,' said Mr Hope. 'He managed to knock a sharp knife off the kitchen table. It caught his back as it fell and gave him a nasty cut that needed a couple of stitches. He's still a bit shaky on his legs so he'll be better staying here overnight.'

Butch was a huge crossbreed dog. 'Poor thing!' said Mandy. 'He's such a softie. I bet he's feeling sorry for himself. I'll pop in and see him before I go to bed.'

But Mr Hope said it would be best to leave Butch to settle. 'You can give him his breakfast in the morning,' he told her. 'We've got a heavy surgery and your mum's going to a seminar in York so I'll be glad of some help.'

Next morning Mandy had just seen her mum off after breakfast on the patio, when Mr Hope came out with some news.

'Dora Janeki's just phoned,' he said. 'Apparently, the Jacob belongs to her new neighbours at Quarry Cottage. But that's the only information I managed to get out of her.'

Mandy smiled. 'It's a good start, though, Dad. But why did Dora phone you? Is there a problem? She hardly ever calls you out.'

'One of her older ewes has just had a lamb,' replied Mr Hope.

'I thought lambs were always born in spring,' said Mandy. 'Not now, in early summer.'

'Hill farmers try to plan it that way,' Mr Hope agreed. 'But Dora hadn't planned on this ewe having a lamb at all so it was all rather a surprise. She says they both seem OK but she'd like them checked over to be sure.'

'So you'll be going up to Syke Farm?' said Mandy.

Adam Hope nodded. 'Yes. I told Dora I'd call in after surgery. You can come with me if you like. If Ken's home you might be able to get a bit more information about the Jacob out of him.' Ken Hudson was Dora's brother. He'd recently moved to live at the farm with Dora.

'Will it be OK if James comes too?' Mandy asked. 'He's bringing Blackie over this morning for his booster.'

'As long as you make sure Blackie stays in the Land-rover when we get to Syke Farm,' warned Mr Hope. 'I know Blackie and Tess are great friends but Whistler doesn't like any other dog on his patch.' Tess and Whistler were Dora's sheepdogs. Tess had been rescued by Mandy and James and Dora had given her a home.

Mandy knew Dora Janeki didn't take too kindly to visitors, either. She just hoped they would be able to find out some more about the blind sheep. She decided to phone James and tell him the news straight away.

'Shall I go and give Butch his breakfast after I've spoken to James?'

Mr Hope nodded. 'Just give him a small portion. He might not eat it. I'm afraid Butch isn't feeling too happy. When I checked him earlier he was trying to bite at his stitches so I had to put a cone on him.'

After preparing Butch's breakfast Mandy spent a few minutes talking to him and stroking his huge, grey head before offering him the meal.

He looked at her with sorrowful amber eyes, then whined and pawed at the white plastic cone round his neck. 'It's OK, Butch,' Mandy told him. 'You'll still be able to put your head down to the dish.' But Butch didn't even try.

'Come on, boy,' she coaxed. 'You must be hungry, a big fellow like you.'

'Don't worry, Mandy,' came a voice from the doorway. It was Simon, Animal Ark's practice nurse. 'Flo's just phoned. She'll be coming to fetch him soon. Butch can have his breakfast at home.'

'That's OK, then,' said Mandy. 'I'll go and see if
Dad wants me for anything.'

'You could help me,' said Simon. 'Walter Pickard's
brought Tom in. Your mum prescribed some
eyedrops for him a couple of days ago, but Walter
can't hold him still long enough to get the drops
in.'

'Uh-oh!' said Mandy. Walter Pickard's Tom was a
big, tough, black-and-white cat – the bully of the
neighbourhood, always getting into fights. Tom
occasionally allowed people to stroke him, but
when it came to being picked up . . . Well, even
Walter had a struggle to do that. 'I guess you'll need
a spot of help,' she added with a smile and Simon
nodded.

A few minutes later, Mandy and Walter were
holding Tom down on the treatment table while
Simon wrestled with the cat's head, trying to keep
it still as Tom hissed and spat.

'I don't think *anyone* could treat Tom single-
handedly,' said Mandy.

'Maybe not,' Walter agreed. 'But I still feel a bit
of a fool having to bring him here to have his drops
put in.'

Walter's voice seemed to soothe Tom a bit. His
body still rumbled with deep moaning noises but

he stopped thrashing around. Simon reached for the eye-dropper he had ready on the treatment tray.

'There!' he said, a couple of seconds later. 'Done! That wasn't too bad after all, was it, Tom?'

Tom yowled and began to wriggle again. Walter picked him up, popped him into the carrier and quickly closed the lid. 'Thank you very much,' he said. 'I'll get off before he can show me up any more.'

Mandy smiled as Walter hurried out with Tom yowling and scratching at the sides of the tough plastic carrier.

'Nice easy one next,' said Simon, as Imogen Parker Smythe came in holding a large cardboard carrier. 'Barney and Button for their vaccinations.'

'Hi, Mandy,' said Imogen. 'It's really crowded out there and one man's got a very fierce dog with him. It kept trying to sniff the carrier. I'm sure he knew there were rabbits inside!'

Mandy smiled at the younger girl. Then she glanced at Simon. 'You don't need me, do you? I'll go and see if Dad needs any help.'

Mandy noticed Sam Western in the waiting area with one of his bulldogs. Mandy thought he might have been the man Imogen had been talking about.

Mr Hope was just wiping down the treatment table when Mandy went in.

'It's Mr Western next,' he told her with a rueful smile.

'He only needs some more of those eardrops you gave him before,' snapped Sam Western when he marched in. 'I told your receptionist when I phoned that there was no need for you to see him again.'

'It may not be the same trouble he had last time,' Mr Hope replied. 'It's better to check these things.'

Mr Western lifted the dog on to the table. 'Freeze!' he ordered harshly. The dog glared his dislike at Mr Hope, but he sat still while the vet examined his ear.

'I'm afraid it isn't the same problem at all,' said Mr Hope. 'He's got a nasty infection here. He needs an antibiotic injection.'

The muscular bulldog winced when Mr Hope injected him. If it had been any other dog, Mandy would have stroked it. But she couldn't chance it with one of Sam Western's dogs!

Just as he was leaving, Sam Western asked Mr Hope if the new people at Quarry Cottage were clients. When Mr Hope said he hadn't met them yet, the other man strode out, adding over his shoulder, 'Well, *whoever* their vet is, something needs to be done!'

'Dad! Do you think they're neglecting their animals?' Mandy demanded. 'After all, they haven't asked you to look at the Jacob and there's something wrong with it.'

'Calm down, love. There might be another vet caring for the Jacob. Or, more likely, Sam Western could be trying to stir things up. The people at Quarry Cottage caused him trouble over the quarry that hasn't been filled in, remember?'

But Mandy was still worried when James came in with Blackie later that morning. 'Do you need me any more, Dad?' she asked, when Mr Hope had given Blackie his injection.

'No, it's OK. I've only got a budgie's beak to clip now,' he said.

Mandy hustled James out. Then she told him what Sam Western had said about the new people at Quarry Cottage. 'I know Dad's probably right and it's just Sam Western's way of trying to get even,' she said. 'But what if they *are* neglecting their animals, James?'

'I doubt they are, Mandy. But they clearly need some help with their animals. Let's wait and see what we find out from Dora. Then we can decide what we should do,' said James.

Mandy nodded. 'OK. How about having a game of ball with Blackie until Dad's ready? It'll help pass the time.'

James agreed with a grin. He knew Mandy always hated waiting.

Syke Farm stood high on the moorside, three miles from Welford village. In winter it was a bleak and desolate area. Today, though, the sun was shining, the steep surrounding hills were purple with heather and the curlews were calling.

But, whatever the weather, Dora Janeki always looked miserable. She was small and wiry and wore her grey hair pulled straight back off her wrinkled face. Her nose and her eyes were sharp. Mandy thought they seemed even sharper than usual as she glanced across to the barn where Dora stood, hands on hips, waiting for them to get out of the Animal Ark Land-rover.

'There's Whistler,' said Mandy, as she and James followed Mr Hope across to the barn. 'No sign of Tess, though. Maybe she's out with Ken.'

'Whistler's very quiet,' said James, looking across at the tall, rangy, grey-coated sheepdog. Whistler usually growled and snarled at anyone who set foot in his farmyard.

'Dora probably told him to stay quiet,' Mandy replied. 'But he does look a bit sorry for himself.'

'If you're coming, get a move on!' Dora snapped

from the barn door. Mandy and James quickened their pace and stepped inside.

The old ewe seemed to be as proud as anything of her lamb. It was skipping round her and giving high-pitched bleats. Neither lamb nor ewe seemed at all bothered when Mr Hope walked towards them.

'The old 'un was hand-reared,' said Dora. 'Never seems to forget that. Comes running up like a dog whenever she catches sight of me. Didn't mean for this to happen,' she added. 'I thought she was past it.'

Mandy smiled as her dad lifted the lamb and put it on a bale of hay. She'd seen lots of newborn lambs but she still felt the same thrill every time she saw one. Apart from its dark brown eyes and short black eyelashes, this one was white all over and its woolly coat looked like fluffy cotton wool.

The ewe watched calmly as Mr Hope examined her lamb. He was smiling, too, and Mandy knew her dad felt the same way she did. 'She's as fit as a fiddle,' he told Dora.

Dora nodded sharply and gathered up the lamb. Then she turned to Mandy. 'Here,' she said. 'Hold her while your dad looks at the ewe.'

Mandy was surprised and delighted. She looked

down at the small animal wriggling in her arms and smiled up at James. 'Isn't she gorgeous?' she said.

'Yes, she is,' James agreed. He moved closer to stroke the lamb's face and Mandy laughed as it sucked hard at his finger.

'You know what, Mandy?' James murmured after a couple of minutes. 'She's closed her eyes. I think she's fallen asleep.'

Mandy nodded and glanced over towards Dora. She was longing to ask her about the new people at Quarry Cottage, but she knew she'd have to wait until her dad had finished examining the ewe.

'No problems here, either,' said Adam Hope. 'She's got plenty of milk and there's no soreness on or around her teats. You can give the lamb back to her now, Mandy.'

Mandy gave the lamb one last quick cuddle before putting it down. She was surprised to see that Dora was watching her with *almost* a smile on her stern face.

Now! thought Mandy, taking a deep breath. 'Dad says the Jacob sheep James and I saw yesterday belongs to your new neighbours.'

Dora sniffed and nodded. 'Weird folk with weird ideas.'

'What other animals have they got?' Mandy asked.

'None as yet,' Dora snapped. 'And they should get rid of that sheep. It's nothing but a menace! Breaks out all the time and makes straight for one of my champion shearing gimmers . . .'

Mandy threw a puzzled look at her dad. 'That's a sheep between its first and second shearing, before it's had any lambs,' he told her.

'Who,' Dora continued grimly, 'insists on looking after the darned Jacob. Seems to know it needs help because it's blind.'

'Do you know if she has always been blind, Dora? Was she born blind or did something happen?'

Dora glared at Mandy and lifted her thin sharp shoulders in an irritated shrug.

'But her owners *know* she's blind?' said James.

Dora glared at James then, giving another of her sharp nods. 'And that's enough of them. Can do without new folk with fancy ideas!'

James blushed. Mandy threw him a sympathetic smile and gave a small shrug as they followed Dora out of the barn. They obviously weren't going to get any more information out of her.

Dora closed the barn door, turned to glance over at Whistler and clicked her fingers. The sheepdog started moving towards them, but he was limping badly.

'He's hurt!' gasped Mandy.

'Hmm! I thought it had gone to rights,' Dora pursed her lips as they watched Whistler approach. 'He started going a shade lame on that back leg after he'd been running,' she told Mr Hope. 'It lasted about twenty minutes or so then went back to normal. Happened three or four times, but yesterday he was fine. There was no sign anything had been wrong.'

Adam Hope bent to speak soothingly to Whistler, and ran his fingers over the sheepdog's body, then down his back legs. 'Has he caught his side against a wall when he's been jumping over it, or anything like that?' he asked.

'Now you mention it, he took a nasty knock from one of the rams a couple of weeks back,' said Dora. 'He didn't seem to be hurt though.'

'I think the impact of the knock must have caused him to jerk sharply and that's caused damage of some kind to the muscles round his backbone,' said Mr Hope, straightening up.

'Damage of *some* kind?' snapped Dora. 'Is that the most you can say?'

Mandy opened her mouth to protest but thought better of it and clamped it shut. She glanced at her dad, read the meaningful look he gave her, and guessed he wanted to talk to Dora.

'I'll give him an anti-inflammatory injection. While I do it why don't you two take Blackie for a walk down the track?' her dad said. 'I'll pick you up at the top of the bridle-path in about twenty minutes.'

Four

'Your dad's a terrific vet!' James exploded as they walked away from the farm. 'Dora's got a real nerve speaking to him like that!'

Mandy nodded. 'But she's probably worried, James. I know people say she's a bit of a skinflint but I don't think she's got much money. Tess isn't fully trained yet. If Whistler got too bad to work she'd have to buy another sheepdog, and a good one costs a fortune.

'Still,' she continued, 'Dad didn't look too concerned. I'm sure he'll sort something out for Whistler. Meanwhile, we've got time to go down the track and wander past Quarry Cottage.'

'And if Dora's neighbours are around it would be rude if we didn't go and introduce ourselves,' said James, catching Mandy's eye. The plan was beginning to take shape.

'And if they aren't outside, I suppose we could go and knock on the door and ask for a drink of water,' Mandy suggested.

'That's a bit feeble,' said James.

'Well, you think up a better excuse,' Mandy challenged him, as Blackie tugged James over to a cluster of heather.

She watched the Labrador as he sniffed and scrabbled eagerly. 'Let him off the lead, James, till we get closer to Quarry Cottage,' she suggested, and Blackie woofed happily as if he were showing approval.

As they made their way along the rutted track, with bracken growing tall and green at either side and clumps of tussocky grass waiting to trip the unwary, Mandy wondered what they could say if they saw one of Dora's new neighbours. How easy would it be to mention the blind sheep?

Suddenly James touched her arm and pointed. 'Look, Mandy!' he said.

There was a figure with its back to them, wearing frayed denim shorts, a T-shirt and a baseball cap, crouching down at the far side of a concrete path that ran down the centre of the big fenced field at the front of the cottage. And, Mandy noticed suddenly, in front of the figure was the Jacob sheep!

'Cripes!' said James, running forward. 'Blackie's making straight for them. Blackie! Blackie! Here, boy!'

But Blackie kept going and only came to a halt when the figure turned and held out a hand to him. Blackie greeted her like a long-lost friend, and Mandy and James glanced at each other in astonishment. It was Harriet Ruck. But what was she doing here with the blind sheep?

As Mandy and James drew closer, Blackie left Harriet and ran up to James who quickly clipped on his lead. Harriet rose to her feet, took a couple of steps back and put her hand on the sheep's neck. Then she stared at the two friends, her eyes dark and brooding.

'Hi, Harriet,' said Mandy, ignoring the unfriendly look. 'Whatever are you doing here? Did you find the sheep wandering around? She's really gorgeous,' Mandy went on, without giving Harriet time to answer. 'Do you think she'll let me stroke her?'

Harriet shrugged and Mandy crouched down in

front of the sheep. 'Hello,' she said softly. 'It's OK, I'm a friend too. Smell my hand. That's right. Oh, you're so beautiful. Come and see her, James.'

James moved forward and bent down next to Mandy. 'She doesn't look neglected to me,' he murmured. 'Her coat's soft and silky and—'

Before James could say any more, Harriet grabbed the neck of his T-shirt and hauled him to his feet. 'Of course Lizzie isn't neglected!' she said, her eyes flashing, her face red with fury. 'Who said she was? The unfriendly farmer woman from Syke Farm? Or that Mr Western who owns the land at the other side of ours? Oh, it's not fair, it's just not fair!'

Mandy's eyes widened. So Harriet and her parents were Dora's new neighbours!

Harriet's anger died as quickly as it had risen. She moved away from James, bent down and buried her face in the sheep's side. The sheep bleated, lowered its head and nuzzled at Harriet's bare knee.

'Oh, Lizzie,' groaned Harriet. 'What *are* we going to do? If only you'd stop getting out and wandering off. Now Mum and Dad—' Harriet broke off from what she had been going to say.

Mandy thought she heard a muffled sob and her heart went out to the other girl. There seemed to be a really special relationship between Harriet and Lizzie. Then Blackie whined and pulled free of his lead. He went and sat down next to Harriet, pushing his big black face into hers.

She must be OK if both Blackie and Lizzie like her so much, Mandy told herself, watching as Harriet put an arm round Blackie's neck. 'Harriet,' she said, 'why don't you tell us about it? James and I love animals and we'd like to help if we could.'

Harriet looked up. 'What could *you* do?' she asked scornfully. 'Make everybody suddenly be friends with us? Make my parents see that it wasn't a mistake taking on a blind sheep?'

To Mandy's surprise James spoke up. 'If you ask me, you aren't giving anyone a chance to be friends with you.'

Blackie whined and snuggled closer to Harriet. 'And *you're* a traitor,' James told him. 'You didn't bat an eyelid when she grabbed me.'

A small giggle escaped from Harriet. She stood up and looked James straight in the eye. 'I'm sorry about that. And you're quite right, I'm not giving anyone a chance to make friends. It's just that . . .' Harriet took a deep breath, 'We've only met Mrs Janeki from Syke Farm, Mr Western who owns a quarry down there, and a man who works for him.

And they've *all* been unfriendly.'

Mandy supposed she could understand Harriet's attitude now. Harriet probably thought everybody round Welford was the same! 'And I expect Lizzie keeps making things worse by escaping and going off with one of the sheep from Syke Farm?' Mandy said aloud.

Harriet nodded. 'She got out twice yesterday. The first time I managed to get her back before Mum realised. That's what made me late for the trip.'

'Then the second time she made her way to the gliding club,' said James.

'With Mrs Janeki's sheep!' said Harriet. 'I didn't *dare* tell anyone Lizzie was mine. I didn't want my parents or Mrs Janeki to find out about it.'

Mandy asked Harriet what she'd meant about her parents thinking it had been a mistake to take on a blind sheep. 'Hasn't she always belonged to you?'

'And what happened to make her blind?' asked James.

'See the grey specks on her eyeballs?' said Harriet. 'They're scars. Some thorns scratched her eyes when a dog chased her into a thicket of brambles.'

'The thorns must have stuck right in!' said Mandy,

stroking the trusting black-and-white face that was turned towards her.

'Dad saw it happen from the car. The dog chased her across the road in front of him and Lizzie ran right into the middle of the thicket. Dad said it took him ages to get her out. The farmer who owned her came along just as he'd got her free. Dad asked where his farm was and a couple of weeks later we called in to see how Lizzie was.'

Harriet took a deep breath and her eyes flashed with anger again. 'The farmer said he was going to get rid of her because the thorns had caused so much damage she'd be blind. But I think she can see a bit with her left one. Anyway,' she added, turning to rub Lizzie's forehead, 'we were due to move in here, so I managed to persuade Mum and Dad to think about buying her for me.'

'Good for you!' said James.

Harriet explained that first her dad had taken Lizzie to an animal hospital to see a vet who specialised in eye problems. He hadn't been able to do anything but he'd said Lizzie was fit and healthy in every other way. He'd thought it was worth giving her a chance to learn to cope with her blindness.

'But,' sighed Harriet, 'I had to promise that if

she didn't settle in, or if being blind made her
unhappy, we'd have to let her go . . .'

Harriet crouched down and stroked Lizzie's neck.
The sheep gave a small bleat, moved her head
round and pushed her nose into Harriet's face.

Mandy felt tears well up in her eyes. 'I think she
knows you're doing your best for her, Harriet,' she
said softly.

'Yup. She obviously trusts you,' said James.

'But she doesn't seem to be settling,' said Harriet.
'Mum and Dad think we should try and find somewhere else for her. But who else would want to take
on a blind sheep?'

Lizzie bleated and pawed the ground. 'I'm sure she knows this is her home,' said Harriet. 'She wants to go back in. Do you think you could help me carry her over the cattle grid? And would you come and meet my mum to let her see that some people round here *are* friendly?'

'Of course we will,' said Mandy, wondering if there might be anything she could say to persuade Mrs Ruck to give Lizzie a bit longer to settle in. She also wondered if she'd have time before she and James had to go back to meet up with her dad.

'You don't *have* to,' Harriet said in a stiff little voice, as she noticed Mandy glancing back up the track.

She still isn't sure that we really want to be friends, thought Mandy. Then she explained quickly, 'My dad's at Syke Farm. We're supposed to be meeting him at the end of the bridle-path. I was just checking to see if I could spot the Land-rover.'

'It's not there yet,' confirmed James.

'Dad's sure to guess where we are anyway,' said Mandy. 'C'mon, Harriet. We really would like to meet your mum. Wouldn't we, James?'

James nodded.

'OK,' said Harriet. 'Will Blackie walk over the grid, James?'

'No way,' James replied. 'We'll have to carry him over as well.'

'I'll come and help you with Blackie when we've carried Lizzie over, James,' Mandy said.

Harriet looked down at Lizzie who was nibbling at some juicy grass growing at the edge of the cattle grid. She lifted the sheep's head then gently nudged her round until she was facing in Mandy's direction.

'You take her front end and I'll take her back, then we'll walk over sideways,' said Harriet. 'Lift on the count of three, OK?'

Mandy nodded, bent down and put her arms either side of Lizzie's chest. But just as Harriet said 'three', Lizzie decided to nibble Mandy's hair.

Mandy started giggling and forgot to lift. 'She's tickling me,' she gasped, looking up at Harriet. Then she giggled all the harder. Harriet had started to lift the sheep and she looked as if she couldn't make up her mind whether to stop or to carry on.

'It's like you're trying to lift a wheelbarrow that's too heavy for you!' Mandy spluttered. 'Oh, Harriet, if you could have seen the look on your face!'

Harriet lowered Lizzie's back legs to the ground. 'Well, you should see *your* face!' she laughed. 'There's bits of the grass Lizzie was nibbling all over your right cheek!'

Mandy wiped a hand across her cheek and moved Lizzie's mouth from her hair. 'Right,' she said. 'Let's try again.'

'OK,' said Harriet. 'One . . . two . . . three . . .'

This time both she and Mandy lifted at the same time. 'I didn't think she'd be as heavy as this!' Mandy panted as they staggered across the grid.

James started to applaud as the girls lowered Lizzie to the ground and Lizzie turned her face in his direction.

Mandy ran her fingers through Lizzie's coat. 'It's so soft. It's much longer than it is on other breeds,' she said.

Harriet nodded. 'It will grow even longer than this. The farmer sheared her before he let us take her. All Jacobs are pretty,' she added. 'But I think Lizzie is one of the prettiest I've ever seen.'

James cleared his throat loudly.

'Sorry, James. I'm coming now.' Mandy hurried back across the grid then she and James carried a squirming Blackie over.

'You can let him off the lead, if you like, James,' said Harriet. 'The fields are fenced or hedged all round, so he won't be able to get out.'

'How does Lizzie get out then?' he asked.

'That's a real mystery,' Harriet sighed. 'She seems

to get out by magic whenever Millie's around.' Harriet pulled a face, 'I don't think Mrs Janeki is the sort who approves of giving sheep names, but that's what I call Lizzie's friend.'

'Dora Janeki's not so bad when you get used to her,' said Mandy.

'She almost smiled when she was watching you with that lamb earlier,' James recalled.

'Has she got a sick lamb?' Harriet asked. 'Is that why your dad's there, because he's the vet?'

Mandy told Harriet about Dora's old ewe and added, 'Both my parents are vets.'

'Lucky you,' said Harriet. 'I bet you know lots of people.'

'*You* know us now,' said Mandy. 'And I'm sure you'll soon make other friends.'

'I think Lizzie and Blackie are going to be good friends,' said James laughing. 'Just look at them.'

Blackie had his nose to the ground, sniffing out this new area, but every so often he moved his big head to rub it against Lizzie's, who was walking as close to Blackie as she possibly could.

Suddenly, though, Blackie picked up a really exciting trail and started to move faster. Bleating a protest, Lizzie ran too.

'Cripes!' gasped, James, pointing to a line of

sheets that were flapping in the wind. 'They're heading straight for the washing!'

Harriet shrieked out a warning as her mother suddenly came round the corner of the cottage carrying a plastic laundry basket.

Blackie would probably have stopped in time if Lizzie hadn't barged against his side. The Labrador gave a startled yelp and they both fell against the wooden clothes-prop. Mrs Ruck yelled as both the prop and the clothes-line snapped and one of the big sheets that had been on the line draped itself over her, covering her completely.

Blackie yelped again, this time in excitement. Mrs Ruck had dropped the empty laundry basket and the wind was blowing it all over the place.

Blackie lolloped after the basket, leaping up and pawing it to the ground. He managed to pick it up then he ran back towards Mrs Ruck with it. But the basket slowed him down and James grabbed him just before he reached the sheet-shrouded figure.

Harriet and Mandy just managed to avoid falling over James and Blackie as they dashed to help Mrs Ruck untangle herself from the sheet.

By now, Lizzie was standing a short distance away, bleating loudly.

'Harriet!' Mrs Ruck spluttered from inside the sheet. 'That sheep has got to go!'

Five

'Oh, no, Mrs Ruck!' James dashed over to help. 'It was Blackie's fault. Please don't make Harriet get rid of Lizzie. It's not fair to blame—' He broke off suddenly, his face as red as a beetroot. 'Sorry,' he mumbled. 'I didn't mean to be rude.'

Mrs Ruck had the same dark hair and dark eyes as Harriet. *And she's just as fiery too*, thought Mandy, as Mrs Ruck, free of the sheet, put her hands on her hips and glared at her daughter.

'I mean it, Harriet! It just isn't working out. Where was she this morning when you found her? In with Mrs Janeki's sheep?'

'She was only a little way down the track,' Harriet

said. 'On her own. Nobody saw her. Well, only Mandy and James and they helped me get her back in. Mandy's parents are the local vets.'

Mrs Ruck ran a hand through her hair and sighed. Then she glanced at Mandy and James. 'You must think it's me who's being rude,' she said with a tight smile. 'I didn't mean to ignore you. It's just that Lizzie is causing so much trouble.'

She looked over to Lizzie who was still bleating loudly. 'For heaven's sake, will someone take her over to the water and give her a drink? That should calm her down.'

James sped away, glad of an excuse to be on his own for a minute or two.

'Here, I'll help pick up the washing,' said Mandy, reaching for the laundry basket. 'Then we'd better go. Dad might be waiting for us.'

Harriet's face clouded. Mandy searched her mind for something – *anything* – she could say in Lizzie's favour before she and James left. Then she heard the Animal Ark Land-rover coming down the track. Maybe . . .

Mandy took a deep breath. 'Would it be OK if I asked Dad if he can think of anything that might help Lizzie to settle in, Mrs Ruck?' she said.

'I doubt he'll be interested in our problems, Mandy,' she replied crisply.

'He's seen you! He's turning in!' Harriet said in triumph, waving her arms at the approaching vehicle.

Mandy wasn't going to give Mrs Ruck the chance of forbidding her to say anything to her dad. 'Fetch Lizzie, Harriet,' she urged, as she dashed forward to meet him.

Adam Hope didn't have a chance to get out of the Land-rover before Mandy told him the whole story at full speed. She ended breathlessly with, 'So, can you think of anything that would help Lizzie? She's so beautiful,' she added, as James and Harriet came up to them, leading the Jacob along by one horn.

'And if you can,' Mandy whispered urgently as Mrs Ruck hurried towards them, 'will you tell Harriet's mum what it is?'

Then Mandy made the introductions and gazed at her dad with pleading eyes.

'Can you help, Mr Hope?' asked Harriet.

Mrs Ruck sighed in exasperation. 'I'm sorry about this, Mr Hope. We really don't want to burden you with our troubles. But if you know anyone who could cope with a blind sheep who can escape from places it should be impossible to escape from . . .'

Harriet drew a horrified breath. Mandy moved closer to her and met James's eyes. This wasn't going the way she'd planned at all!

Adam Hope stroked his beard thoughtfully, his eyes on Lizzie. 'She is a beauty,' he said. 'I think, though,' he went on carefully, 'she's probably lonely for other sheep. It isn't often a sheep is kept on its own.'

'Do you mean Lizzie will only settle if there are other sheep to keep her company?' Harriet asked.

'I'm sorry, Harriet,' Mr Hope replied. 'It's no help to you, but I do think that's likely to be the case.'

Mandy felt terrible. She'd been trying to help and she'd only ended up making things worse. But to her astonishment, Harriet gave a small shriek of delight.

'Well, it's sorted then, isn't it, Mum?'

'I suppose it could be,' Mrs Ruck agreed. 'But we'll still have a couple of weeks to get through, Harriet.'

'Harriet?' Mandy and James spoke together, both totally bewildered.

Harriet spun round to face them. 'We're getting a small flock of Wensleydale sheep soon,' she said, her eyes sparkling.

'That's brilliant!' Mandy laughed.

'Are you going in for breeding Wensleydales, Mrs Ruck?' Adam Hope asked. 'You've certainly enough land here. It looks like good grazing too.'

'We probably will breed from them but that isn't our main reason for getting our own flock,' Mrs Ruck replied.

'Can we take them in and show them, Mum?' Harriet asked.

'Mr Hope probably hasn't got time right now, Harriet,' Mrs Ruck replied. 'But,' she added, looking up at him, 'you'd be very welcome to come and see our set-up whenever you like.'

Mr Hope glanced at his watch. 'I have got a few minutes to spare,' he said.

So Mrs Ruck led the way into the cottage, through the kitchen and into the large front room.

Harriet pointed to the shelves that completely lined the two longest walls. On one lot of shelves were cardboard boxes full to the top with skeins of wool. The second set of shelves held neat piles of sweaters, hats, gloves, scarves and socks.

'Mum and Dad have people who knit these for us,' Harriet explained. 'And they sell them all over the world.'

'At the moment we buy fleeces at wool auctions,

then send them to be spun,' said Mrs Ruck. 'Mostly, we use wool from Swaledale sheep for knitting winter sportswear.'

'Famous explorers have worn gloves and hats knitted by Mum and her knitters,' Harriet told them proudly.

'Wow!' said James, impressed. 'You mean explorers in the Arctic and places like that?'

Mrs Ruck nodded and smiled at Mr Hope. 'Gordon and I have about twenty knitters working for us. But wool is very fashionable now, and there's a demand for knitwear using finer, softer wool. We both took a course on spinning some time back and we bought an old spinning-wheel that we're having restored. We want to start spinning wool ourselves, from our own sheep.'

'That's why we moved here,' said Harriet. 'There's enough land to keep a small flock of sheep and there are two big barns. One for the spinning and one for the sheep.'

'*Now* I see why you're going in for Wensleydales, Mrs Ruck,' said Adam Hope. 'Heavy fleeces with a sheen to the wool.'

'Yes. We're getting them from Gordon's uncle who's having to sell up to make way for a new road.'

'I used to spend most of the school holidays

there,' said Harriet. 'That's how—' She stopped abruptly. But Mandy guessed she'd been going to say that's how she knew about rounding up sheep.

'He's getting on a bit,' continued Mrs Ruck, 'so he decided to retire instead of starting over somewhere new.'

'That's where Dad is now,' said Harriet. 'Looking at the Wensleydales and deciding how many to get. And trying to persuade Aunt Pamela to be one of our hand-knitters.'

Mrs Ruck went on to explain that all their knitters were dalesfolk. 'Mainly farmers' wives or retired people,' she said. 'The problem is, it's a winter-only job for the farmers' wives and there just aren't enough of them to keep us ahead on our orders. We were hoping we might find some knitters here, but I've got a feeling people in Welford won't approve.'

'They'll probably come round soon enough,' said Mr Hope. 'After all, you're reviving an old dales tradition. I can remember my grandmother knitting socks and gloves from local wool.'

'I'll have to tell Mum about these,' said James, pointing to a pile of sweaters. 'It's Dad's birthday soon and she was wondering what to get him. Would it be OK if she came to look at them, Mrs Ruck?'

'Of course it would, James,' Mrs Ruck nodded. 'And if you know anyone who likes knitting, send them along too.'

'Mum meant what she said about people who like to knit,' said Harriet a few minutes later. Mandy was stroking Lizzie, and James was untying Blackie's lead from the hook in the wall near the water trough.

'Mum and Dad are worried that we'll get our sheep and then not have enough people to knit the wool we'll get from them,' Harriet continued. 'But when Mum mentioned the problem to Mrs Janeki, *she* said that folk round here had better things to do with their time.'

'We'll ask around,' promised Mandy. 'I'd love a sweater knitted from your wool, Lizzie,' she said, rubbing the Jacob's soft neck. 'She really is terrific, Harriet.'

Harriet nodded. 'Apart from the trouble she causes. I get really worried in case something happens to her when she wanders off.'

'I'm sure everything will be OK,' said Mandy.

'Will you bring Blackie to see her again soon?' asked Harriet. 'He'll help her not to feel so lonely until the new sheep arrive.'

'You bet we will,' said James. 'And I'd like to see your parents' spinning-wheel.'

'No problem!' laughed Harriet. 'I'm sure they'd love to give you a demonstration.'

'Right now, Dad's demonstrating that it's time to go,' said Mandy, as Mr Hope caught her eye and pointed at his watch. 'We'll see you soon, Harriet.'

'And you, Lizzie,' said James, giving the Jacob one last stroke before hurrying after Mandy.

'They both look much happier than they did when we arrived,' Mandy commented, waving to Harriet and Mrs Ruck from the Land-rover window.

'Yes, they're having a few problems settling in,' said Mr Hope. 'But I'm sure things will work out well for them in the end.'

'Dora Janeki might be a bit friendlier towards them if Lizzie stops leading her prize sheep into mischief,' said James.

'Yes,' Mr Hope agreed. 'Dora's got enough to do without having to worry about that.'

'What about Whistler, Dad? Is he going to be OK?'

'Me being on the spot certainly saved Dora a journey to Animal Ark,' Adam Hope said. 'The anti-inflammatory injection I gave Whistler should relieve any swelling and pain round the muscles that were jarred and I've told Dora to rest him for two or three days. I think he'll be all right, although Dora isn't too happy about not being able to work him. It's a busy time for sheep farmers.'

Mandy grinned. 'If Dora saw us visiting her weird neighbours and finds out that we're planning to help Mrs Ruck find some knitters she won't be too happy about that, either!' she said.

'I didn't know we were planning that,' said James. 'Oh, no,' he added. 'Something tells me you've got one of your ideas.'

Mandy nodded. 'I have. But you'll have to wait until tomorrow to hear about it, James.'

Grandad was just coming out of his shed when Mandy and James arrived at Lilac Cottage the following day.

'Hi!' Mandy called.

'Mandy!' said Grandad. 'And James, too. This is a nice surprise. I'm always glad to see you, but today I'm *especially* glad. You might be able to help Gran forget her troubles for a while.'

'Why? Is something wrong with her?' Mandy asked in alarm.

'Nothing that finding someone to give a talk in the WI tent at the Country and Agricultural Show wouldn't cure,' Grandad replied. 'It seems as if nobody's free on the date Gran needs them.'

The show was held every year in the large park close to where James lived. As well as competitions for sheep, goats, dogs and poultry, there were stalls selling local goods, and activities and workshops relating to country and farming life. The Women's Institute always had a large tent where someone gave a talk or a demonstration. People paid to go in and the money raised went to charity.

'We came to ask for Gran's help,' said Mandy. 'But I guess we'll be able to help her out too. We know just the person to solve her problem. Don't we, James?'

James glanced at Grandad and nodded.

'Oh, no.' Grandad smiled at James and winked. 'Has she got one of her ideas, James?'

'I'm afraid she has, Mr Hope,' said James.

'Hey! Stop talking about me as if I'm not here!' Mandy protested. 'Anyway, it's a brilliant idea, James. You know it is!' Then she saw the look on their faces and laughed.

When they went inside, Gran was sitting at the kitchen table surrounded by magazines. 'I didn't hear you come up the path,' she said, jumping up to give Mandy a hug. 'I was searching through these magazines, trying to find someone, *anyone*, I could book for the WI tent.'

'No need, Gran,' said Mandy. 'James and I are here to help.'

'I'll put the kettle on while they tell you about it, Dorothy,' said Grandad. 'I hope these two have solved your problem. Life can get back to normal then.'

'Did you know some new people had moved into Quarry Cottage, Gran?' asked Mandy.

Gran shook her head. 'I'd heard it was sold,' she said. 'But that's all.'

'Well, their name's Ruck and they've got a blind Jacob sheep called Lizzie.'

'I might have known an animal came into it somewhere,' said Grandad. 'All right, all right, Dorothy, I'll let her get on with it,' he said quickly when Gran threw him a look.

With James's help, Mandy went on to tell her grandparents all about Lizzie, the Rucks' knitting business and their plans for spinning their own wool from their own sheep.

'So we think,' Mandy ended, with a triumphant smile, 'that Mrs Ruck would be really interested in giving a spinning demonstration and a talk about knitting.'

'It would help her get to know people as well,' said James.

Mandy nodded. 'And maybe some of the WI members would be interested in knitting for her, Gran. That's what we came to ask you. But, when we heard about your problem, we realised maybe we could solve both at once!'

'I think it's a marvellous idea!' Gran said. 'I'll phone this Mrs Ruck right now and see if she's willing to do it. Better yet, I'll pay her a visit. Introduce myself and make her feel welcome.'

'I'll drive you up there, Dorothy,' Grandad offered. 'Get it sorted and settled. And I daresay you two wouldn't mind seeing Lizzie again,' he added, smiling at Mandy and James.

Six

'There's no sign of Lizzie,' said Mandy, as Grandad drove slowly over the cattle grid and down the path towards Quarry Cottage.

'Maybe they've shut her in the barn so she can't get into any mischief,' James suggested. 'Anyway, here's Harriet's mum.'

'Hello, Mrs Ruck!' said Mandy. 'James and I have brought my grandparents to see you. Gran's got something special to ask you.'

'That sounds intriguing.' Mrs Ruck smiled at Gran and Grandad. 'I'm Prue Ruck. Come on in.'

After they'd all introduced themselves and made

their way to the back door, Mandy asked where Harriet was.

'Out with her dad looking for Lizzie,' Mrs Ruck replied.

'Cripes!' said James. 'Lizzie's as bad as Houdini!'

'Houdini's a goat,' Mandy explained. 'He used to escape all the time until Lydia Fawcett had her top meadow fenced off.'

'Lizzie *didn't* escape this time,' Mrs Ruck told them. She glanced round at her visitors with a rueful smile. 'I had a whole van-load of cardboard boxes delivered. After we'd unloaded them the van driver told me that when he'd driven in there'd been a stray sheep on my land. He said it was panicking because it couldn't get back over the cattle grid to the one waiting on the other side.'

'I bet that was Millie!' said James. The man didn't . . . ?'

'You guessed it!' said Mrs Ruck. 'The silly man picked Lizzie up and carried her across the grid! He was so proud of himself because he'd managed to catch her all on his own! Of course,' she added, 'by the time he told me, Lizzie and her friend were nowhere in sight.'

'But what did the foolish chap think the cattle

grid's there for?' asked Grandad, shaking his head.

'I asked him that,' said Mrs Ruck. 'He thought it was there to stop sheep coming *in*. I suppose it's understandable. Not many people have just one solitary sheep. And of course he could see all the other sheep up on the moors.'

Mandy glanced at her grandparents. 'Is it OK if we go and look for Lizzie, too, while you're talking things over with Mrs Ruck?'

Gran nodded and Mandy and James dashed off.

As they got close to the bridle-path leading down to Syke Farm they saw Ken Hudson approaching it from the opposite direction. He was striding along with Tess at his heels.

Ken said something to Tess, and the next second the dog was racing towards them, her tail held high and wagging crazily.

'Tess! Hello then. Who's a good dog?'

Tess didn't jump up. She slowed to a halt and stood looking at them, her eyes bright, her tongue lolling out of one corner of her mouth. Mandy and James petted her while they waited for Ken to catch her up.

James greeted Ken and told him about the van driver carrying Lizzie over the cattle grid.

Ken gave a snort and said, 'Well, she's not up on

the top moors. I've just come from there. Didn't see any sign of a Jacob.'

Mandy gazed around wondering which way she and James should go.

'It's likely she's gone along one of the sheep tracks,' said Ken. 'Especially if she's with that gimmer of Dora's who's taken up looking after her.' Ken gave Mandy a knowing look.

'We think she might be, but we weren't going to mention that,' Mandy admitted.

Ken smiled. 'Try the track up there on the right by the hawthorn hedge. There's a stile at the end. She could have come up against that and stopped there.'

'That's a good idea. Thanks, Ken,' said Mandy. They said goodbye to him and Tess and hurried off.

'Good thing it was Ken we met and not Dora!' said Mandy as they turned on to the narrow sheep track that wound its way between two moorland meadows rising up on either side. Just then, a rabbit appeared round the bend. For a second, the startled creature froze. Then, with a twitch of its whiskers and a flicker of its tail, it crossed the footpath, bounded halfway up the sloping edge of the meadow and stopped. After a moment or two another rabbit popped out of a nearby burrow. Then the two of them started a crazy game of dodge and chase. Mandy and James stood still to watch and Mandy noticed ears and faces popping up from other burrows on the slope.

But something must have startled them because, as quick as a flash, all the rabbits suddenly disappeared.

Then the silence was broken by a familiar voice that rang out clearly from round the bend. 'I'm sure there'll be something we can do, Dad. They're not very deep scratches.'

'That's Harriet!' Mandy gasped. 'Quick, James. Lizzie must be hurt!'

They ran so fast they almost careered straight into Harriet, Lizzie and Mr Ruck as they all rounded the bend at the same time.

'Harriet! What's wrong?' Mandy bent down and looked anxiously at the Jacob.

'Lizzie's OK. She was standing by the stile at the end of the footpath bleating her head off,' said Harriet. 'Millie was with her but she made her way up the slope to the meadow when Dad and I arrived.'

'That's OK, then.' Mandy let out a sigh of relief.

'Are you sure she's all right?' asked James. 'We

heard you talking about scratches . . .'

Harriet grimaced and James and Mandy followed her gaze to the big, blond-haired man standing behind Lizzie. He was frowning as he looked at the pair of spectacles in his hand.

'It's the lenses of Dad's glasses that got scratched,' Harriet explained in a tight little voice. 'Lizzie caught them with her horns when he bent to turn her round.'

There was an awkward little silence, then James spoke up. 'There's a good optician in Walton, Mr Ruck. It wouldn't take long to fit new lenses if you need them.'

Harriet threw James a grateful look. 'And you can stop my pocket money until they're paid for, Dad,' she said.

Mandy noticed that Mr Ruck wasn't looking quite so annoyed and decided to take the chance of speaking up in Lizzie's defence. 'I think the delivery man who carried Lizzie over the grid should pay for them,' she said.

James nodded in agreement.

Mr Ruck eyed them sternly. 'You two are as bad as Harriet,' he said. 'The fact remains, if Lizzie hadn't been by the grid . . .' Then his face broke into a smile. 'OK, I agree it wasn't entirely her fault this time. Let's get her home.'

Mandy shot a quick look of triumph at James. They'd help to win this battle, anyway!

As they started walking, Lizzie gave an occasional low bleat. 'I think she knows she's going home,' said James. Lizzie turned her head in his direction and gave a louder bleat.

'Do you think she's wondering where Blackie is?' he asked. 'We'll bring him with us next time, Lizzie.'

'Why didn't you bring him with you?' Harriet asked.

'We hadn't planned on coming,' said Mandy. Then she went on to explain why they'd come.

Mr Ruck was very enthusiastic. 'If my wife doesn't want to give a talk, I'll offer to do it,' he said. 'It might help the people round here to realise we aren't "townies" come to live in the country to play at being sheep farmers.'

Harriet sighed. At least Mandy's family and James didn't think that.

'Mandy's gran will soon have everyone wanting to meet you and see what you're doing at Quarry Cottage,' said James, as Mr Ruck carried Lizzie over the cattle grid.

Over an hour later, when they finally left Quarry Cottage, Mandy smiled at her friend as Gran said virtually the same thing. 'And as soon as I get home I'm going to start on some large posters advertising Prue's talk,' she added.

'That's great, Gran. James and I could put one on the big notice-board by the park gates.'

'Grandad will drop one off first thing in the morning,' said Gran. She turned in her seat to wink at Mandy. 'I'm sure he'll be taking himself off on his bike for the day so that I can't get him writing posters, too!'

'You bet I will,' agreed Grandad, and they all laughed.

'Mandy! Harriet's on the phone,' called Mrs Hope. Mandy was giving her three pet rabbits their breakfast and she quickly shut the hutch door and leaped up.

Harriet phoning this early can only mean one thing! she said to herself as she raced up the garden and into the kitchen. *Lizzie must have got out again!*

'Don't panic,' said Harriet when she heard Mandy's anxious voice. 'It's good news. The spinning-wheel's just arrived and I couldn't wait to tell you! If you and James want to come up, Mum'll give you a demonstration.'

'We'll come right after we've put up a poster for

Gran,' said Mandy, glancing at the colourful poster Grandad had dropped off earlier.

There were already a few posters advertising events at the show when Mandy and James arrived at the park gates. 'Here's a good spot for Gran's,' said Mandy.

When they'd pinned it up, Mandy stepped back to make sure it was straight. 'Look at this one!' she said. 'It's advertising a competition to find the most appealing sheep. The winner will have its photo taken and it'll go on the front of a Yorkshire dales sheep calendar. Harriet's just got to enter Lizzie,' she said enthusiastically. 'I'm sure she'd win!'

'The entry forms are in the park-keepers' office,' said James, reading the information at the bottom of the poster. 'We can get one and take it up to Quarry Cottage with us.'

Harriet must have been watching for them because she ran to meet them as they were carrying their bikes over the cattle grid.

Mandy told her about the calendar competition and James handed her the entry form. 'Wow! Let's enter Lizzie!' Harriet laughed. 'But don't mention it to Mum or Dad yet,' she said, as they walked towards the barn. 'I'll wait and choose the right moment.'

Mr Ruck was kneeling over a fleece spread out on a sheet on the grass outside the barn. By his side were a few cardboard boxes with bits of fleece in. Harriet said they were called locks.

Mr Ruck greeted Mandy and James and explained that he was pulling the wool from the fleece and sorting it into different grades before preparing it for spinning.

Harriet picked three locks out of one of the boxes and passed one each to her friends. 'Teasing is one way of getting locks ready for spinning,' she said. 'You hold the lock in your left hand and pinch and pull at it with the thumb and forefinger of your right hand.'

But Mandy and James soon discovered that pulling apart the strands of wool was more difficult than Harriet had made it appear. After a while, Harriet giggled and said, 'I think you both need more time to practise. Come on, Mum's already got a good supply of locks.'

They stopped for a moment to pet Lizzie, who was sitting by the barn door, then followed Harriet in.

Mrs Ruck showed them the spinning-wheel. 'It's

quite an old one but they've made a good job of restoring it. You're just in time to watch me join a new lock on to this length of wool called the "leader" wool.'

Mrs Ruck explained she had to treadle to turn the wheel so the leader wool could wind on to the bobbin.

To Mandy's amazement, Harriet's mum was barefooted. 'I find it easier to work the treadle with bare feet,' she said.

She started to treadle and James and Mandy watched the leader wool begin to wind round the bobbin. When it was almost completely wound, Mrs Ruck picked up some teased wool in her left hand and joined some of it to the end of the leader wool.

As she continued to treadle, they saw the teased wool and the leader wool twisting together to make the join firm. Holding the join with her right hand and treadling gently all the time as she fed the teased wool from her left hand, she made it move forward through the forefinger and thumb of her right hand until all the teased wool had been spun and wound on to the bobbin.

'You keep joining on more wool until the bobbin's full,' she said. 'Then we use a machine to ply two, three or four strands of wool together, to give different thicknesses of wool. The wool is washed, and sometimes dyed, before going to our knitters.'

James was fascinated by the spinning-wheel and wanted to know more about how it worked. Mandy wanted to get the hang of teasing the locks, so she and Harriet took some outside and talked happily, making plans for entering Lizzie in the competition.

They had a late picnic lunch in the meadow and when Lizzie appeared with pieces of teased wool all over the ends of her horns even Harriet's mum and dad laughed.

'It sounds as if Mr and Mrs Ruck are beginning to feel a bit happier,' said Adam Hope when Mandy told them all about her day. The family was sitting out on the patio chatting and enjoying the last of the sun.

Mandy nodded. 'And this is a lovely end to a really good day,' she said, glancing around in contentment.

But a little while later, just as Mandy was about to go up to bed, Harriet phoned. 'Lizzie's been missing since eight o'clock,' she said tearfully. 'Dad and I went looking for her but we couldn't see her anywhere. He won't let me look any more now it's getting dark. And Mum says if Mrs Janeki or anyone

else sees Lizzie and complains, then Lizzie will have
to go!'

Mandy's heart lurched. 'I'll phone James and we'll
come up first thing in the morning,' she promised.
'I'm sure we'll find her before anyone has time to
see her. So try not to worry too much.'

Mandy was frowning when she replaced the
handset. She knew Harriet *would* worry. She was
worried too!

'Problems?' asked Mr Hope.

Mandy nodded and told him what had happened.

'Well, I don't mind you going to help look for
her in the morning,' said Adam Hope, 'but I want
your promise that you won't try to interfere with
any decision Harriet's parents might come to.
Understand?'

Mandy knew her dad meant exactly what he'd
said. She gave him her word and went to bed feeling
more worried than ever about Lizzie's future.

Seven

It was still early when Mandy and James arrived at Quarry Cottage the following morning. 'But not early enough by the looks of it,' James muttered, as Dora Janeki walked out of the Rucks' back door, looking grimmer than ever.

Mandy's eyes met James's in a worried glance as they heard Harriet shouting, 'She must have got out through a hole or a gap and *that* isn't my fault. It's yours!'

Mr Ruck's stern tone reached them as he spoke Harriet's name and Mandy kicked at the ground. She didn't like the idea of walking in on an argument. But they simply had to find out what was going on.

Just then, Harriet flew out of the cottage, her eyes black and stormy, her face ghostly white.

'Harriet!' Mandy moved swiftly towards her. 'Have you found Lizzie? Was she with Dora's sheep? Is that why Dora was here?'

Harriet shook her head, sniffed and dashed a tear from her cheek. Then she explained in a terse little voice that Lizzie was still missing. Worse still, so were four of Dora Janeki's flock. Dora had brought her sheep down off the moor at about six-thirty the previous night to pen them, ready for dipping this morning.

'But she thinks the sheep must have stayed back from the rest without her dog noticing,' Harriet explained. 'She said that's because it wasn't Whistler working them. It was her other dog and she isn't as good. Mrs Janeki didn't realise there were any missing until this morning.'

'Well, the only thing to do is to go looking for them,' James said sensibly. 'If we can bring them all safely home, Mrs Janeki might calm down a bit.'

'But Mum and Dad won't,' Harriet sighed. 'They'll send Lizzie away. I know they will. But you're right, James. We've got to find them!'

After they'd searched every single narrow path leading off the track, and all the lower moorland meadows, they started to make their way on to higher ground. It was hard going. The sheep tracks and footpaths were narrow and rutted with tussocky grass, gorse and heather on either side.

Every now and then one of them stopped and raised their eyes upwards, hoping for a glimpse of sheep in the distance. But there were no white shapes moving among the purple heather on Upper Syke Moor. Mandy turned to the other two with worried eyes. James took his glasses off and rubbed them hard with his T-shirt.

'I think I know what you're going to say,' he told Mandy.

'Me, too,' Harriet agreed. 'But we *mustn't* think the worst. They wouldn't knock a wall down and get on to the gliding club's land *twice*.'

But putting their thought into words made them feel worse. Their alarm lent speed to their feet as they sped up the moorside. They reached the summit of the lower moor and bounded and leaped recklessly down the other side towards the flat plateau and the outer perimeter of the gliding club's land.

It was easier now, running on the flat. They

made for the long drystone wall. It was too high
for them to see over ... but they didn't need to
see. They could hear sheep bleating, and raised
voices.

They scrambled up the wall and down the other
side. There were two men darting around, flapping
their hands and shouting at Lizzie and Dora Janeki's
sheep. One of the men was Mr Ingrams, the gliding
club manager. He looked up and saw Mandy, James
and Harriet.

'Do something quickly!' he yelled urgently,
pointing skywards. 'Look!'

'Cripes! There's a glider. It must be coming in to
land!' gasped James.

Harriet took control. She rattled out instructions
and Mandy and James moved in the direction she
told them to.

The three of them had just got the sheep bunched
together when Mr Ingrams and one of the other
men shot towards them yelling frantically.

They looked behind them. The glider was coming
right at them. They could see the pilot's distorted
face as he pulled hard on the joystick, trying to
gain height. Then Mr Ingrams and the other man
pushed them to the ground.

'Lie flat!' Mr Ingrams called. 'And keep your

heads down,' he added harshly as Harriet raised hers to look up at Lizzie.

Mandy grabbed Harriet's hand and held it tight. Then she felt James's arm come over her shoulders. Mandy could feel it trembling and she knew James was as frightened as she was.

The glider was so low they felt the draught and heard a swishing noise as it passed over them.

Then Mr Ingrams let out a deep sigh of relief and scrambled to his feet. But a second later he groaned. 'He's going to hit the wall!'

Mandy, James and Harriet knelt up, their eyes wide with fear, as they watched the glider getting closer and closer to the long wall opposite the one they'd climbed over.

'It's OK . . . the nose is rising . . . he's going to clear it, Josh!' said Mr Ingrams' colleague. And the glider dropped down and landed on the low part of the slope on the other side of the wall. 'You lot stay put!' Mr Ingrams ordered as he and the other man dashed off towards the glider.

They couldn't have stood up yet, even if they'd wanted to; they were trembling too much. Harriet leaned forward to bury her face against Lizzie's side. Millie and Dora's other sheep had their heads down, grazing without concern.

Mandy was the first to get to her feet. The pilot was getting out of the glider. She held her breath, waiting to see if he was hurt. Then he started shouting and it was clear that he wasn't. But Mandy felt sure she recognised the voice and she glanced fearfully at James and Harriet as they stood up.

Mandy's fear was confirmed when the pilot took off his helmet and goggles. It was Sam Western!

The three of them watched nervously as a long and heated discussion took place. Then the men climbed over the wall. Mr Ingrams came towards them while Mr Western strode furiously towards the clubhouse with the other man.

'You'd better make yourselves scarce,' Mr Ingrams said, eyeing them grimly. 'And take these sheep with you.'

'How did they get in?' asked Mandy. 'How do we get them out?'

Mr Ingrams looked uncomfortable. 'There's a sheep hole in the wall you climbed over,' he said, pointing. 'Somehow we must have missed blocking it up. Get them out as quickly as you can. I'll see if I can calm Mr Western down but I doubt I'll be able to. He had a very narrow escape! We all did!'

Harriet was too upset to speak. She took hold of Lizzie's left horn and guided her towards the wall.

Mandy and James didn't really have to do anything about Dora's sheep. They just followed Lizzie and Harriet, and went through the sheep hole in the wall without any hesitation.

On the other side of the wall, Harriet said, 'I'll stay in front with Lizzie. You follow with the others.'

It was obvious she didn't want to talk. Mandy and James didn't feel much like talking, either. They felt tired and weary and were still shaken up by what had happened. Occasionally, they murmured a word when one of Dora's sheep moved off or stopped to graze; but they didn't do that often. The sheep seemed to know they were going home.

An hour or so later, when they reached the cattle grid leading on to the Rucks' land, Harriet turned. 'Will you take Dora's sheep to her? I'll wait here for you.'

But Lizzie suddenly baa-ed loudly and jerked herself away when Harriet took hold of one of her horns. Millie made a series of low, rumbling bleats in reply. The sheep behind her stopped.

Mandy could hardly believe what happened next.

One of Dora's sheep lay down close to the edge of the cattle-grid. Two others came to either side of her, lowered their heads and nudged her shoulders, pushing her until her body covered the

spaced-out bars of the grid. Then Millie nudged Lizzie to turn her so she was facing the grid.

Everything was taking place so quickly and had taken them by such complete surprise that they couldn't do a thing to stop it. They only had time to gape and stare unbelievingly as Millie pushed Lizzie gently over the sheep who was lying on the grid, its body acting as a bridge to the other side.

As soon as Lizzie stepped off the prone sheep's tail end on to the path, the sheep dragged itself along by hooking its front feet over each bar in turn, using each one for leverage.

'I can't believe it!' James muttered as the sheep

got to its feet and shook itself before going to stand with the others.

'Here's Tess!' said Mandy.

'And Mrs Janeki!' Harriet gasped. 'Do you think she saw?'

'If she did, I doubt she'll admit it,' said Mandy. 'Lizzie must get out that way too. Which means Dora's sheep are responsible. But I don't think we'd better mention it right now,' she added in a hasty whisper as Dora got close.

Dora called a low command to Tess and the dog got behind the sheep, making them run up the track towards Sykc Farm.

'I've had a phone call from Sam Western!' Dora snapped. 'He's on his way here and I'll be back when I've penned the sheep.'

'Let's get Lizzie into the barn before Mr Western gets here,' said Harriet, bounding across the cattle grid.

'And let's tell your parents *how* Lizzie gets out,' said Mandy.

Harriet told them her dad wasn't home. He'd gone to buy some fleeces.

'Well, we'll tell your mum,' said James. 'And we'll tell her about the sheep hole the gliding club didn't block up, as well!'

Mrs Ruck listened carefully to what the three of them told her, but when they'd finished she shook her head.

'It doesn't make any difference,' she said. 'It's still Lizzie being here that causes the trouble.'

She turned to Mandy. 'Your father phoned a while back to see if there was any news,' she said. 'There wasn't then but I asked him if he'd find somewhere for Lizzie to go. He said he'd call in after lunch.'

Before anyone could say anything, they saw Sam Western's car coming down the concrete path. As he got close they saw his livid face and could see that Mr Ingrams was with him.

James nudged Mandy and, to her relief, she saw the Animal Ark Land-rover turning in just as Sam Western leaped out of his car, followed more slowly by Mr Ingrams.

'I won't spend any time on this, Mrs Ruck,' Mr Western grated, standing close to her in a hector-ing, bullying way. 'I own the gliding club's land. That blind sheep of yours was on *my* landing field and almost caused a fatal accident.'

Mr Hope got out of the Land-rover in time to hear Mr Western's last words. He glanced at his daughter with raised eyebrows – asking silently for confirmation.

'It's not fair blaming Lizzie for it all!' Mandy said indignantly. 'Someone should have made sure that sheep hole was blocked off. That's how Lizzie and Dora's sheep got in, Dad!'

'Quiet, child!' Sam Western ordered. Then he turned back to Mrs Ruck. 'If you won't agree to getting rid of that blind sheep, I'll shoot it,' he snarled. 'And I've every right to do so!'

Eight

Harriet buried her face in her hands and began to sob. Mandy took a step towards her friend then stopped as Mrs Ruck began to speak.

'Now you listen to me, Mr Western!' she said, her eyes bright with anger. 'You seem to be remarkably slack when it comes to attending to things on your land. You leave the quarry unfilled, with no safety barriers around it, no warning notices or anything . . .'

Harriet lowered her hands and gazed at her mother in astonishment.

James caught Mandy's eyes and mouthed the word 'Wow!'

And Mrs Ruck continued in an angry but quiet voice, '. . . You say the gliding club land is yours. That means the responsibility of making sure the sheep can't get in is also yours. So before you come here with your threats again, you go and put your own affairs in order!'

With that, Mrs Ruck turned and walked into the cottage, closing the door firmly behind her.

Sam Western turned to Mr Hope. 'Get your vehicle out of my way,' he said. 'I'm leaving. But you can tell that woman that she hasn't heard the last of this by any means. And as for you . . .' he added, as Dora Janeki strode towards them, 'if you'd complained a bit harder when that blind sheep started breaking out, all this could have been prevented.'

Dora eyed Sam Western grimly before turning and going back the way she'd arrived – over the wall that split off her land from the Rucks'.

Adam Hope drove the Land-rover on to the field at the side of the path.

Mr Western, followed by Mr Ingrams, who had remained silent throughout, got into his car, and drove to the bottom of the path where he could turn round.

Mandy, James and Harriet watched him go, then

Mandy ran over to her dad. 'We know how Lizzie gets out,' she said, and proceeded to tell him. 'It's true,' she added. 'Honestly, Dad.'

Mr Hope nodded. 'I have heard of that happening once before,' he said. 'I would have loved to have seen it myself.'

'And,' Mandy continued, 'I know I promised I wouldn't interfere, but . . .'

'Does Mrs Ruck know how Lizzie's been getting out?' asked Mr Hope. Mandy nodded. 'All right,' he said. 'Harriet, how about you going to ask your mum if I can have a word with her?'

Harriet dashed off and reappeared a few minutes later with her mother.

'If you still feel the same way and you want me to help you to find a new home for Lizzie, I'll try,' said Adam Hope. 'But . . .'

Mandy clenched her hands into tight fists as she waited to hear what her dad would say next.

'. . . your Wensleydales will be here in a few days,' he continued. 'I still think they'll help Lizzie to settle. And Mandy's just told me how she's been escaping. It seems the blame isn't all hers.'

'So it appears,' Prue Ruck agreed. 'OK, so we'll give Lizzie another chance. And,' she admitted, 'it will show Sam Western that I will *not* be ordered around by a bully like him.'

Harriet gave a shriek and hugged her mum tightly.

'OK. OK,' Mrs Ruck said. 'But listen, Harriet. Lizzie's a bigger responsibility than ever now. I don't think Mr Western would have a right to shoot her if she got on to his land again. But I don't think that would prevent him from doing so,' she added grimly.

'I'll keep Lizzie shut in the barn until our other sheep arrive,' promised Harriet. 'I'll even sleep in the barn with her if I have to,' she added fiercely. Then she burst into tears of joy and relief.

'Oh, Harriet!' Mrs Ruck shook her head and held Harriet close.

'Come on, you two,' Mr Hope said quietly. 'Put your bikes in the back and we'll leave them to it, hmm?'

'I'll certainly be glad to get home,' said James as they drove off. 'I'm going to have a shower, make a huge sandwich and then I'm going to lie in the garden for the rest of the day.'

'And you've got a special job to do back at Animal Ark,' Mr Hope told Mandy. 'A couple of young cats have been brought in for spaying tomorrow. I think they could do with a spot of your TLC.'

Mandy smiled. Her parents often said her tender loving care was as good as a tonic. Reassuring two worried cats would be just the thing to calm her down after everything that had happened.

'Mandy! Have you seen this?' It was two days later and James burst into Animal Ark's kitchen, waving a copy of the local newspaper. 'Look!' he said putting the paper on the breakfast table and jabbing a finger at the headline:

JACOB SHEEP JEOPARDISES GLIDER PILOT'S LANDING!

Mandy gasped as she started to read furiously down the column. Adam Hope got up and stood behind her chair, reading over her shoulder.

'I *bet* Sam Western gave them the story,' said James. 'His name's mentioned three times in the article!'

Mandy nodded. 'And just read this bit at the end, Dad! "In spite of neighbouring farmer, Mrs Dora Janeki, having many times asked Mrs Prudence Ruck to ensure her one and only sheep, a blind Jacob, does not escape, her requests seem to have fallen on deaf ears. The Jacob continues to cause disruption to Mrs Janeki's working day and large flock of commercial sheep. But perhaps now that it's been seen that the Jacob could put human lives at risk, Mrs Janeki's problems will be over".'

Mandy threw the paper down in disgust and looked up at Mr Hope. 'Dad, when I told you what Dora's sheep did at the cattle grid, you said it wasn't unusual—'

'No, Mandy,' he interrupted. 'I said I'd heard about it happening once before.'

'OK. So what if I phone the newspaper and tell them that it's Dora Janeki's sheep who help Lizzie to get out?' she said.

Adam Hope threw her a sympathetic look. 'I know how you feel, love. But it wouldn't be a good idea. It still boils down to the same fact in the end. It's Lizzie being there and wanting to get to Dora's sheep that causes the disruption.'

'That's what my parents said when they read this,' James admitted.

'But . . . isn't there *anything* we can do, Dad?'

'Yes. Just leave things as they are and hope that Lizzie settles down when the new sheep arrive. I'll have a word with the Rucks later and suggest that they put collars and bells on the Wensleydales.'

'So Lizzie will be able to hear them moving

around?' said James. 'That's a great idea, Mr Hope.'

'Right. So forget about trying to stir things up, Mandy. Agreed?'

'OK,' she said. 'But we'll go and see Harriet. She'll be really upset if she's seen the newspaper.'

As Mandy and James hurried towards the Rucks' cottage, the sound of bleating and baa-ing filled the air. 'It sounds too close to be Dora's sheep,' said James. 'It's coming from the barn. The Wensleydales must have arrived.'

But when they went into the barn only Harriet and Lizzie were there.

'What was all that bleating?' asked Mandy, gazing around in puzzlement.

Harriet gave a tight smile and waved a hand towards a cassette player. 'It was a tape,' she said. 'Dad suddenly remembered he'd bought it a couple of years ago. It was made by a shepherd who'd recorded his flock of sheep bleating because it sounded like they were singing. Dad thought it might help Lizzie settle down if we played it to her.'

'Does she like it?' asked James, going over to stroke the Jacob. 'Do you, girl?' he said, as Lizzie turned her face towards his and rubbed against him.

'I don't think so,' Harriet sighed. 'She kept

running round in circles trying to find *real* sheep.'

Mandy watched as Harriet stroked Lizzie's forehead. Their new friend looked so sad. She was doing her very best for Lizzie but everything seemed to be going wrong.

'Have you seen the local paper?' Harriet asked, looking up suddenly.

Mandy nodded. 'That's one reason we came,' she said. 'We knew you'd be upset if you saw it.'

'Dad's really *angry* about it,' Harriet went on. 'But Mum's upset. She phoned your gran and cancelled the talk for the WI, Mandy. She says she won't be able to face anyone. I'm beginning to wonder . . .' Harriet gulped and buried her face against Lizzie's side, '. . . maybe we *should* try to find a new home for Lizzie,' she whispered. 'Mum didn't suggest it, but I think she might be able to face people if they knew Lizzie was going. We could put a notice in that horrible newspaper and everyone would see it!'

'But, Harriet, the other sheep are coming soon,' said Mandy. 'If your parents still agree, I think you should wait and see if Lizzie settles down.'

'Me, too,' said James. 'You can't give up, Harriet!'

'OK,' said Harriet. Then she sighed as Lizzie bleated and moved restlessly round the barn. 'But she hates being shut in,' she sighed. 'Look at her! Even with us here, she's miserable. She doesn't mind being in here at night but she knows it's day-time now.'

'How about putting a collar and lead on her and taking her out?' James suggested. 'I could go and fetch an old one of Blackie's.'

'I promised I'd keep her shut in here until the other sheep come,' said Harriet. 'I wish we could borrow a sheep from somewhere to stay in here with her. She might not mind so much then.'

'Let's make her one!' Mandy said suddenly.

James and Harriet exchanged a startled glance. What on earth was Mandy talking about?

'Remember that model farm we made when we were in primary school, James?' asked Mandy. 'I know it was a long time ago,' she added, giggling at the look on her friend's face, 'but we made some sheep out of cotton reels and bits of sheep wool. Why don't we make a sheep-sized version as a friend for Lizzie?'

'We'd need to find loads of wool to make a big one!' Harriet protested.

'No, we wouldn't, Harriet,' said James, suddenly seeing that Mandy's idea could work. 'Not if your dad brought some fleeces home yesterday.'

'He did,' said Harriet.

'Well, we could wrap one round something and—'

'We could use a small bench for the body,' Harriet interrupted, her face alight with enthusiasm. 'Or better still . . . Listen! Dad's got an old sawhorse somewhere. You know, the sort of bench you rest wood on to saw it? The bench part is like a body, with four sloping legs – so it looks a bit like a horse.'

'You mean a bit like a *sheep*!' cried Mandy. 'That'd be just the thing. We could fix the fleece around the body and—'

'A cardboard box would do for the head,' said James. 'We'd have to put the fleece over that as well.'

'And we could stick small bits of fleece on the saw-sheep's legs,' said Mandy. 'Are you listening, Lizzie?' She cuddled the Jacob close. 'We're going to make you a friend!'

They set to work, and in a couple of hours they'd finished making Lizzie's friend. Harriet went to fetch her parents.

'I hope they won't think we're interfering too much, James,' Mandy said anxiously.

'Mmm, I know what you mean,' he replied, his eyes on Lizzie. 'But I think it will be OK when they see that.'

Mandy followed James's gaze. The Jacob was

rubbing her body against the fleece-covered sawhorse. 'I expect you're right, James. Lizzie looks happier already.'

Nine

When Mr and Mrs Ruck came in to the barn, they stared in amazement at Lizzie and her companion. 'Whose idea was this?' Mrs Ruck asked at last.

'Mine,' Mandy mumbled. 'I hope you don't mind.'

'But I thought of using your sawhorse to make it, Dad,' said Harriet.

'So *that*'s what it is! I knew I recognised the shape but I couldn't work out—' Mr Ruck broke off and shook his head.

'We haven't damaged it,' James said anxiously. 'And we haven't cut the fleece. It is OK, isn't it?'

'I think we're very lucky to have such good friends,' Mrs Ruck replied. 'I only wish one of us

had thought of something like this when we first got her. It might have saved a whole lot of trouble.'

Suddenly, Gordon Ruck burst into laughter. 'I'm sorry,' he spluttered, 'Lizzie looks so ridiculous making friends with . . . that *thing*!'

The others joined in with his laughter. They were laughing so hard they all turned in surprise when they noticed a persistent knocking at the barn door.

Mr Ruck went to open it. Mandy was surprised when she saw who'd been knocking. 'It's Mrs Spiller and Jenny from Fordbeck Farm,' she told Mrs Ruck. 'Jenny's got her own pet lamb.'

'Mandy! James!' Little Jenny Spiller ducked under

Mr Ruck's arm and ran towards them. 'I wanted to see the blind sheep,' she said. Then her eyes went big and round as Mandy moved back and pointed to Lizzie.

'She's beautiful,' she said. 'Can I stroke her?'

'Of course you can,' said Harriet. 'And her friend as well,' she said solemnly and Jenny gave a delighted giggle.

'Jenny saw the word "sheep" in the paper and made me read the story to her. She wouldn't give me a minute's peace until I agreed to bring her,' Mrs Spiller told the Rucks. 'I hope you don't mind. Besides, I wanted to tell you to let me and my husband know if you need any help with anything.'

'I've come to see if you need any help as well,' came a voice from the barn door. Lydia Fawcett walked in and introduced herself to the Rucks.

'I saw the newspaper story and thought Sam Western was probably behind it. I've had a couple of disagreements with him in the past,' she explained, glancing across at Mandy and James, who'd been involved in them. 'I might have known you two would be here!' she added with a smile.

'This is very kind of you all,' said Mrs Ruck. 'I'm beginning to think Welford isn't such a bad place to live after all.'

'I'm really looking forward to your talk at the show,' Mrs Spiller told her. 'Mandy's gran mentioned it at our meeting last night. I love knitting and it will be really interesting to watch wool being spun. I just see it in the fleece stage when we're shearing,' she said with a smile. 'I don't know anything about what happens to it next.'

Lydia looked puzzled, so Mandy told her all about the Rucks' knitting business. 'Hmm,' said Lydia. 'I've been toying with the idea of breeding a few Angora goats for their wool. I think I'll have to talk it over with Mr and Mrs Ruck!'

'So . . .' Mandy told her parents later on, '. . . Lizzie loves her new friend. I'm sure she'll be OK once the Wensleydales arrive and she's got *real* sheep for company.'

Mandy turned to Gran, who'd popped into Animal Ark with some vegetables from Grandad's garden. 'And, thanks to Mrs Spiller and Lydia, Harriet's mum *will* still give the talk, Gran.'

Gran nodded. 'I know, love. Prue Ruck phoned back to tell me. She got on like a house on fire with Lydia and Maggie. She's found some new friends and I think Maggie is going to be the Rucks' first local knitter.'

'It's all good news, Mandy,' said Mr Hope. 'But remember, if Lizzie *doesn't* settle . . .'

'I know, Dad. She's on her last chance. But the Rucks' new sheep are due tomorrow and I've got a feeling everything will be OK then.'

A couple of days later, Mandy and James went home with Harriet after school. When they arrived, the new Wensleydale sheep were wandering contentedly around the large field in front of the cottage, stopping every now and then to graze or chew the cud.

Harriet's parents had taken Mr Hope's advice and the sheep were all wearing collars with bells on. Most of them had been sheared before they'd arrived but there were some that hadn't been.

'The smaller ones are only eight months old,' Harriet told them, smiling at the look of delight on her friends' faces. 'So they didn't need shearing.'

'They're beautiful!' said Mandy. She thought they looked as if they'd been to the hairdresser's. Their wool was long and crimped and fell over their eyes and bluish faces in twisty strands like a long fringe.

'Has Lizzie made friends with any of them?' James asked.

'Well,' Harriet replied, 'she looks up when she

hears their bells ringing or when they bleat. I think she feels more at home knowing they're here, but she doesn't seem to have made any special friends yet.'

'Maybe she prefers Jock,' grinned James as they walked closer to the cottage where Lizzie was grazing with the sawhorse sheep close to her side.

Harriet called the sawhorse sheep Jock because the fleece they'd used was from a Scottish Blackface sheep.

'She looks terrific, Harriet,' Mandy said, rubbing the Jacob's neck.

Harriet nodded proudly and said she was grooming Lizzie every day, brushing her coat, and rubbing her hooves and horns to make them shine. 'But,' she added with a sigh, 'Mum and Dad aren't too keen on the idea of taking her to the show because Dora Janeki and Mr Western are sure to be there. Mum thinks Lizzie should keep a low profile.'

'Nobody can complain about Lizzie getting out any more,' said James. 'She's as good as gold now.'

'Except for when she wanders into the kitchen,' Harriet laughed. 'She came in while I was making my sandwiches for school this morning and helped herself to a slice of bread off the table. So who knows what she'd get up to at a show!'

'We'll help you talk your mum round, Harriet,' said Mandy.

James nodded. 'We will!' he agreed.

'I heard that!' laughed Mrs Ruck. She'd come up behind them without being seen. 'Mrs Spiller came to see the Wensleydales this morning,' she went on. 'And *she* said Lizzie should be entered in the calendar competition, too! What with her and you three . . .'

'Does that mean we *can* enter her, Mum?' Harriet looked up with a hopeful smile.

'I'm still a bit dubious about it in case Mr Western causes a scene. But I suppose, if it means that much to you—'

'Fantastic! Thanks, Mum!' said Harriet.

'We'll make sure she behaves herself, Mrs Ruck,' said James.

'She's so beautiful, and her coat's growing back quickly,' Harriet said happily. 'She might even stand a chance of winning!'

'Her coat has grown,' said Mrs Ruck. 'It's about time we dipped her. The Wensleydales were dipped before they came so, as we'll only have Lizzie to do this time, we'll use an old tin bath.'

'I know dipping sheep is important, but I don't exactly know *why* it is,' said Mandy.

Mrs Ruck smiled and told them that bathing sheep in a special solution helped to control diseases like sheep scab. 'That's a very unpleasant skin irritation caused by mites getting under the sheeps' skin,' she explained. 'And dipping helps discourage other nasty things like lice and blowfly that live on sheep if they get the chance.'

'So when will you be dipping her?' asked Mandy eagerly. 'Do you think we could come and help, Mrs Ruck?'

'You have to wear special clothing while you're dipping,' said Harriet. 'Rubber suits, goggles and a mask and wellies and rubber gloves.'

Mrs Ruck nodded. 'The chemicals can be very dangerous for humans,' she said. Mandy and James looked disappointed. 'But,' she added with a smile, 'as long as you make sure to stay well away from the tin bath, you can come and watch. If it's fine tomorrow, we'll do her then.'

'Wow! That'll be great,' said James. 'Thanks, Mrs Ruck.'

'These early morning visits seem to have become a habit,' said James, as he and Mandy walked down the track that led to the Rucks' after Mrs Hope had dropped them off.

'James! It's not that early. It's almost nine o'clock.'

James groaned and Mandy laughed. Her friend wasn't always at his best in the mornings. But her smile changed to a frown as she spotted Harriet running madly towards them, looking worried.

'Thank goodness you're here,' she cried. 'Lizzie's got out again!'

'How long has she been out?' Mandy asked when she and James reached their friend.

Harriet shook her head worriedly. 'I'm not sure. But that doesn't matter so much. What does matter is that she's hurt her front leg. Mr Ingrams phoned a couple of hours ago to say he'd spotted Lizzie and another sheep through his binoculars. They were making their way down the lane leading from the gliding club and . . .' Harriet gulped, '. . . Lizzie was limping.

'But,' she continued, 'Dad and I have already searched along the lane and over the lower moors.'

'So where do we look now?' Mandy asked urgently.

'They might have made their way to Dora's lower fields,' said Harriet, 'the ones that spread out across the end of our long front meadow. But,' she added, 'the quickest way of reaching them from here is over the wall and across Quarry Field.'

The wall was about two and a half metres high

but there were enough stones jutting out at angles to make climbing it reasonably easy.

Quarry Field was a large open space with patches of dense areas where trees and bushes grew tangled and tall. The grooves worn by the tyres of the heavy lorries that had once carried stone from the quarry could still be seen, but were nearly concealed by tough-looking grass and thistles. There were stones of different shapes and sizes everywhere. It was a harsh and unfriendly grey-green place and Mandy shuddered as they started walking as fast as they could.

After a while, Harriet stopped dead. 'Listen!' she said urgently. 'Which direction is that bleating coming from?'

'It sounds as if it's coming from over there.' James pointed to the left. 'But it can't be. How would a sheep have got in? The walls are too high.'

'There are big double gates at the far end,' said Harriet. 'Someone could have left them open.'

James scrambled up a pile of boulders and peered into the distance. 'You're right,' he said. 'They *are* open.'

The bleating came again. 'It's not from the left, it's from the right,' said Mandy. 'Do you think it's Lizzie, Harriet?'

'Yes, I'm sure it is! It sounds as if she's in a panic. And . . .' Harriet started to run, '. . . the old quarry is over that way!'

Mandy and James tore after Harriet. Mandy tripped over a loose stone and fell, James half-turned to go back and help her, but Mandy was on her feet in a flash, urging him to keep running. She could hear Lizzie's plaintive bleats over the sound of their pounding feet.

Mandy told herself the bleating wouldn't sound so clear if Lizzie had fallen into the quarry. But she knew that if the blind sheep was close to the edge, she could go over any second!

Keep running, Mandy! she ordered herself, trying to ignore the pain shooting up her knee. Then she saw James swerve suddenly to avoid Harriet who'd skidded to a halt. And James stopped too. *Why have they stopped?* Mandy wondered.

Then she saw, and she stopped too.

Millie was lying close to the edge of the quarry, on her back with her feet sticking up in the air. Mandy had heard her parents talking about 'rigged' sheep. She knew a sheep could die if it fell on to its back and wasn't righted in time.

But they couldn't right Millie themselves because Lizzie was nearer still to the quarry's edge. And if she was startled . . . all it would take would be one step back and she'd be over!

They watched with bated breath. Lizzie was facing Millie's flank and, in between bleating, she was banging her head against the other sheep as if trying to roll her over.

As Mandy crept forward to James and Harriet, something long, low and grey appeared as if from nowhere. It was Whistler, Dora's sheepdog. He sank down to the ground just in front of Harriet and began to wiggle along on his stomach.

Too close! He was going to get too close! But a low whistle sounded from across the other side of the quarry. Whistler lay still, his head pushed forward, his body quivering, and Mandy saw Dora standing on the wall that separated her fields from Quarry Field.

Maybe Lizzie sensed Whistler's presence. Her head rose and she took a step back. They all heard the sound of loose stones bouncing down the quarry. Mandy clutched James's arm.

Lizzie was teetering on the edge. And if they moved a muscle, Lizzie could plunge into the abyss below. Harriet let out a low, desperate cry.

Ten

But Lizzie regained her balance. She lifted one front foot and moved it around. 'She's feeling for Millie,' Mandy whispered under her breath. The Jacob's foot touched the gimmer's side. She put it to the ground, then she lowered her head and butted and pushed against Millie.

It was like watching something in slow motion, Millie's body rocked, swayed and rolled. She was on her side now, but was it too late?

'She's getting up!' said James. 'She's on her feet.'

'Don't go to them, Harriet,' Mandy warned quickly as they heard a low whistle of command from Dora. 'Leave it to Whistler and Dora.'

Whistler rose fluidly to his feet, then slunk
forward, taking a wide, silent circle in front of the
sheep. Then he went in behind them. Mandy, James
and Harriet let out huge sighs of relief as the two
sheep moved away from the edge. They were safe
now!

Whistler brought them closer. Lizzie was
hobbling slightly, Harriet called chokily to her and
the Jacob baa-ed long and loud in reply.

'I reckon her bleating was what alerted Whistler
in the first place,' said Dora when she hurried up
to them. 'He knew something was up; wouldn't rest
till I followed him to the boundary wall. The

gimmer will do,' Dora eyed her sheep with a knowledgeable eye.

'Darned nuisance that Jacob may be,' she grumbled on, 'but she can't be blamed for the gates being left open. And,' she added, looking at Harriet, 'happen it's a good thing they've struck up a friendship. Millie, as you call her, is one of the best I've ever bred. Her lambs, when she has them, should sell for a fair amount. She could have died but for that pest of yours righting her.'

Dora gave a low command to Whistler. 'He can keep her there while I . . .' she pulled out a shepherd's knife from the pocket of her jerkin, '. . . make the Jacob's foot more comfortable. I'll trim her hoof back. I reckon she's got a stone stuck between the outer and inner shell.'

Dora lifted Lizzie's foot and expertly began to trim the shell of the hoof. Harriet crouched and rubbed her face lovingly against Lizzie's. Mandy and James kneeled either side of Dora to watch her.

'See?' said Dora, as a small lump of dried soil dropped out. 'I guess that was the culprit. Right, girl,' she lowered Lizzie's foot. 'You'll do.'

'Thank you, Mrs Janeki,' said Harriet.

Dora nodded and straightened up. 'Spent enough

time on all this,' she said. 'I've got work to do, and I want to phone Mr Western about those gates,' she added grimly. 'I'd like to know exactly how they came to be left open.'

James had picked up the lump of soil from Lizzie's hoof and absently rubbed it between his fingers as they walked along. 'Look,' he said suddenly, 'there was a ring-pull off a drink can in the soil. No wonder poor Lizzie was hobbling.'

Dora snorted. 'I can't stand folks who drop litter like that around,' she said.

Mandy shook her head. 'This isn't a ring-pull at all,' she said. 'It's a silver signet ring.' She slipped it over her little finger and showed it to Dora. 'D'you think we should take it to the police station?'

'Could have been lost years ago,' said Dora, 'but you may as well.'

Mandy took the ring off and put it in the zipped pocket of her jeans.

Whistler was a short distance ahead working Millie in the direction of the open gates. Lizzie was walking alongside Millie, with only the slightest hint of a limp, and Mandy nudged Harriet when she saw how Dora was watching Lizzie. But Harriet was tight-lipped and white-faced.

'The Jacob's got looks as well as courage,' said

Dora. 'Happen you've done the right thing, lass, giving her a chance.'

Harriet's eyes flickered but she didn't speak.

'Harriet wants to enter Lizzie for the calendar competition at the show,' said Mandy. 'Her parents aren't too keen on the idea because Mr Western's sure to be there.'

'None of that matters now, does it?' Harriet burst out. 'Lizzie's been wandering again so Mum and Dad will make me get rid of her!'

'That wouldn't be fair!' said James. 'Lizzie doesn't get over the grid by herself. We've seen how it happens!' To Mandy's amazement James swung round and looked fiercely at Dora Janeki.

'Can't stand here gossiping,' snapped Dora, her earlier softer mood deserting her. 'I've still got sheep to dip. Get hold of that Jacob now. I'll get this one back to its rightful place.'

Harriet darted forward and took Lizzie's left horn. Dora whistled a command to Whistler, then turned to Harriet as the sheepdog drove Millie forward. 'I'll be along to speak to your folks later,' she said before striding away.

The three of them plodded slowly back. Tears rolled down Harriet's face as she guided Lizzie along, and Mandy felt like crying in sympathy. But then she glanced at James and saw the determined look on his face. Mandy stopped and turned to face Harriet.

'James and I will stay until Dora Janeki comes,' she said.

'And we'll tell her exactly how Lizzie gets over the grid!' said James. 'I was going to tell her before she marched off.'

'We'll *make* her listen, Harriet!' said Mandy. 'I don't know how, but we will.'

Harriet sniffed. 'I don't think it would do any good,' she said. 'I didn't tell you before because . . . because I think I was trying to pretend to myself that I hadn't heard it. And if I hadn't heard it, it wouldn't happen.'

'Hadn't heard what?'

'What wouldn't happen?'

James and Mandy spoke at exactly the same time.

'After Mr Ingrams had phoned I heard Mum tell Dad she felt like giving everything up and moving to a town,' mumbled Harriet.

'She probably didn't mean it,' said Mandy. 'Maybe she just said it in the heat of the moment.'

But Harriet shook her head and walked on quickly with Lizzie.

Mandy shrugged helplessly and murmured to

James, 'We'll have to see how things look when we get there.'

When they got close to the cattle grid, Harriet stopped and turned to look at Mandy and James. 'See that?' she said on a sob. 'Dad's walking up the path with a pickaxe. I bet he's coming to dig a hole to put up a "For Sale" sign.'

Mandy gasped and, without stopping to think, she bounded over the grid and dashed up to Mr Ruck. 'Whatever Mrs Janeki says, it *is* her sheep who help Lizzie get out. Besides, Lizzie just saved Millie's life and Dora Janeki saw the whole thing!'

Mandy rattled off the story of the rescue, then, after stopping to catch her breath, added, 'Please, Mr Ruck. Please don't give everything up and go! It would break Harriet's heart.'

'Is that what Harriet thinks is happening?' Mr Ruck asked in alarm. 'Does she really think we'd leave all this?'

Mandy nodded and pointed to the pickaxe. 'She thinks you're digging a hole for a "For Sale" board.'

Mr Ruck shook his head. Feeling a spurt of hope, Mandy followed him as he hurried towards Harriet who was lifting Lizzie over the grid with a worried-looking James.

'We're *not* going *anywhere*, Harriet,' her dad said.

'And neither is Lizzie, if I can help it.'

Mandy breathed a long sigh of relief, and James punched the air, grinning.

'What's the pickaxe for then, Dad?' Harriet asked.

'I'm going to make another cattle grid to go next to this one,' Mr Ruck explained.

'So Dora's sheep won't be able to help Lizzie in and out!' said James, grinning at Mandy and Harriet.

Lizzie bleated, but Harriet couldn't seem to manage a smile. 'Do you think Mum's still going to dip Lizzie?' she asked her dad.

Mandy guessed her friend was still worried by what she'd overheard.

Mr Ruck smiled and pointed towards the cottage where a figure looking like a deep-sea diver was placing a zinc bath on the cobbles in front of the barn. 'I didn't have time to tell you earlier but I popped into the Spillers' last night and borrowed their dipping outfits. So what with mine that I won't be wearing today . . . there's one for each of you.'

Harriet gave a whoop of joy and hurtled off down the path yelling to James and Mandy to bring Lizzie.

Twenty minutes later, Lizzie's woeful bleats filled the air as Mrs Ruck lowered her into the zinc bath.

Before covering her face with the face guard she'd told Mandy, James and Harriet what each of them should do.

Mandy and James held Lizzie's head up and Harriet grabbed a broom and sloshed the solution all over Lizzie. The Jacob struggled and protested; it was hard keeping a good grip on her with rubber-gloved hands but they managed.

And, at last, Mrs Ruck nodded. The three friends stepped back and watched as she lifted Lizzie out.

For a split second Lizzie seemed to freeze to the spot on the cobbles. Then, with a long drawn out 'baa-aaa' she shook herself hard before prancing off – kicking her heels together in the air like a playful lamb.

The young Wensleydales joined her, cavorting crazily around the field while the older sheep stared at them scornfully.

The four of them watched the antics for a while before clearing up and getting out of their dipping gear.

Mrs Ruck suggested a picnic lunch and they were all sitting outside eating it when Dora Janeki arrived. Harriet gazed white-faced and huge-eyed at their neighbour.

'Hello, Mrs Janeki,' said Mrs Ruck, getting up

and going forward to meet her neighbour.

Dora nodded sharply, then said, 'That Jacob can travel with my sheep to the show. And if Sam Western has any objection to her being there he can make it to me. I wasn't right happy about that bit in the newspaper. It may have been true but I didn't like the way it was done. Nobody had any right to quote me without my say-so. Which they wouldn't have got.'

It was a long speech for Dora and, for a moment, there was a stunned silence.

Mrs Ruck was the first to find her voice. She thanked Dora then added, 'Gordon's starting on another cattle grid. I don't think we'll have any more trouble with Lizzie getting out.'

'Hard work digging, concreting and laying iron bars,' said Dora. 'I'll ask Ken to come and lend a hand. That's only right, all things considered.'

They all realised that was Dora's way of admitting that she *did* know how Lizzie got in and out, but none of them mentioned it.

Then, with another sharp nod, Dora Janeki turned, and they watched as she climbed nimbly over the boundary wall on to her own land.

'And I thought she'd come to complain!' said Harriet.

The picnic took on a festive air. Lizzie bleated loudly when she heard all the noise so Harriet ran over to get her.

Soon, they were joined by Mr Ruck, and Mrs Hope, who'd driven up to collect Mandy and James.

She had to hear the whole story and when Harriet asked shyly if Mrs Hope would just check Lizzie's foot to make sure it really was all right, Mandy suddenly remembered the silver signet ring.

'We'll drop it off at the police station on our way past,' said Mrs Hope. Then she went over to Lizzie and looked at her foot.

'It's fine,' she assured Harriet. 'She's looking great. I should think she really will stand a good chance in the competition.'

'The show's only a week away, Lizzie,' said Harriet. 'You just make sure you behave yourself until then.'

'*And* while she's there, I hope,' said Mrs Ruck, as Lizzie lowered her head and gobbled greedily at a piece of chocolate cake that had been saved for Mr Ruck. 'She may not be able to see but she can smell bread or cake from miles away. I keep having a dreadful vision of Lizzie at the show, finding her way into the refreshments tent.'

'I promise I won't let her do that,' Harriet laughed.

Mandy and James grinned at each other. They'd do their best to help Harriet keep that promise. But . . . 'Fingers crossed,' Mandy whispered.

Eleven

It's perfect weather for the show, Mandy thought happily as she and James wandered round looking at the stalls while they waited for Dora and Harriet to arrive with the sheep.

It was still early but there were already a lot of people there, and the first of the demonstrations were under way: drystone walling, saddle-making and wood-turning.

James and Mandy stopped for a while to admire a row of shepherds' crooks with sheep or sheepdogs carved on each handle.

And, Mandy noticed with pleasure, there was a nice little crowd round the WI tent where Harriet's mum was setting up her spinning-wheel and a selection of fleeces. They'd offered to help, but Prue Ruck had smiled nervously and said she'd do it all on her own to help calm herself.

Suddenly, James gave a small cry of pleasure and Mandy turned to see Harriet making her way towards them. She was leading Lizzie by her left horn and . . .

'She's got Millie with her, on a lead!' said Mandy, delighted.

Harriet smiled nervously when James and Mandy hurried up to her. 'The calendar competition is being held in that green-and-white tent way over there,' she said. 'Mrs Janeki said I could walk Millie over there with Lizzie, to keep Lizzie calm.'

Mandy smiled. 'Lizzie looks fantastic, Harriet. She's gleaming from head to foot.'

Harriet nodded. 'I rubbed a silk scarf over her after I'd brushed her. I used it on her horns and hooves as well. She does look good, doesn't she?'

'So do the ice creams those kids are eating,' said James. 'The cart's over there. Let's walk that way and get some.'

They chatted happily as they walked towards the cart. Harriet told them that she'd decided Mandy was right about Dora Janeki. She was OK really.

'She even said she'd buy one of Mum's thick sweaters if Millie gets first place in both classes she's entered for,' said Harriet.

'I'll run and get the ice creams while there's nobody waiting to be served,' James said. As he walked away, Harriet felt a sneeze coming on and raised her hand from Lizzie's horn to cover her mouth.

Lizzie baa-ed and, before Mandy or Harriet could stop her, she hurtled off after James.

Mandy yelled; James stopped and Lizzie barged into him, knocking him sideways. He recovered and tried to grab Lizzie but ended up face-down on the ground.

'Oh, no!' yelled Harriet. She thrust Millie's lead into Mandy's hands and dashed forward. Mandy looked frantically round and hustled poor Millie over to a fence, tying her to one of the posts before dashing after Harriet.

They were too far away to get there before the ice-cream seller took one horrified look at Lizzie and fled. A second later the Jacob ran straight into the side of the cart, upending it and its contents all over herself.

From nowhere a small crowd gathered to 'ooh!' and 'aaah!' at the sight of a Jacob sheep standing

happily licking at the strawberry, chocolate and orange sauce trickling down her face and turning her head to gobble at the ice cream running down her sides from the heap on her back.

'What's this sheep doing here?' Sam Western pushed his way through the crowd to take up a threatening stance in front of Harriet and Lizzie.

'I'm entering her for the calendar competition,' said Harriet, facing up bravely to the bullying man.

'You are *not*! This sheep is blind!' he roared at the crowd. 'She's a defective menace. She is constantly wandering around the gliding club's landing field. She's prevented pilots from landing, and last time she was there she nearly caused a glider to crash because it had to swerve to avoid her.'

He swung round to face Harriet. But he slipped on some melting ice cream and landed on his elegantly clothed backside. 'The gliding club and I are going to sue your parents for keeping an animal that puts humans at risk!' he said furiously. 'Get her out of my sight. She's disqualified from the competition.'

Shocked and dismayed, Harriet took hold of Lizzie's horn and pulled her away.

'Do you think he *can* disqualify her?' Mandy asked James.

'I don't know,' said James. 'He *is* wearing a "Show Organiser" badge. Cripes!' he added. 'Dora's pushing her way through the crowd. And does she look angry!'

But to their surprise Mrs Janeki made for Sam Western and glared down at him. 'That's enough of your idle threats, Sam Western!' Dora's voice was cold and hard. 'You'll not find a solicitor in Yorkshire who'd take up a case against a sheep. However, I have no doubt that *I'd* be able to find one easily enough to take up a case against you for failing to have that dangerous quarry filled in!'

'For your information,' blustered Sam Western, 'that is all under control. My men started on the job this morning.'

'There could still be a case to answer to,' snapped Dora. 'I nearly lost my best sheep down that quarry. It's only thanks to the Jacob getting her on to her feet and away from the edge that I didn't. So, Mr Western, just you think long and hard before you try suing anyone!'

'Wow! That's telling him!' James exclaimed, full of admiration for Dora.

Sam Western got to his feet and hurried off, still uttering dire threats.

'Harriet. Go and get that darned Jacob cleaned

up or she'll be too late to enter,' ordered Dora. 'Go on! Get her into the tennis club's changing rooms. There's sure to be a shower in there. You'll have to manage without my gimmer. The judging for her classes is starting soon.'

Mandy darted off to untie Millie and took her over to Dora. Then Harriet tugged gently at Lizzie's horn. 'Come on, Lizzie,' she said.

'What about my cart and this wasted ice cream?' the ice-cream seller called.

Mandy dashed over to the ice-cream seller. 'Harriet's mum is giving a talk in the WI tent and I'm Mandy Hope from Animal Ark,' she told him. 'My dad's here somewhere. He's the duty vet. I'm sure one of them will pay for the wasted ice-cream.'

By now, willing helpers from the crowd had surged forward to right the cart. The nearby refrigerated box on wheels, containing extra supplies, was still intact.

'That's OK, young lady. I reckon we can forget it,' the ice-cream seller winked. 'I've a feeling I'll be selling more ice cream than I would have done before it all happened,' he said. 'Nothing like a bit of drama to whet the appetite!'

'Thanks,' laughed Mandy, and she moved off to follow Harriet, James and Lizzie.

'Perhaps I can help.' A pleasant-looking lady with a small girl by her side touched Mandy on the arm. 'I'm the tennis club captain. I've got the keys to the changing rooms in my bag. You'll need them unlocked if you're going to put the sheep in the shower.'

Mandy's hand flew to her mouth. 'I didn't think about how we'd get in!' she admitted. 'What a good job you're here!'

'No, it's a good job *you're* here,' the lady said with a smile. 'I was going to call in at Animal Ark on our way home.'

'We've got something special to say to the lady who lives at Animal Ark,' said the little girl, smiling shyly at Mandy.

Mandy looked puzzled, but her companion shook her head. 'There'll be time for explanations later,' she said. 'Let's get the sheep seen to first.'

'Is your sheep called Lizzie?' the little girl asked when they caught up with Harriet and James. 'That's what Daddy calls Mummy sometimes. He calls her Elizabeth too, and I'm called Beth.'

Mandy introduced James and Harriet and told them that Beth's mum was going to open up the changing rooms for them.

'How are we going to clean Lizzie without getting

soaked ourselves?' Mandy asked, looking worriedly at Harriet as they walked in.

'No problem,' said James, kicking off his trainers then tugging his T-shirt over his head. 'I'll go under with Lizzie. I can dash home afterwards for some dry shorts.'

'And I'll get the towel from my locker,' said Elizabeth. 'There's only one, I'm afraid, but it's a big one.'

As if to make up for things, Lizzie went into the shower area with no protest at all.

'I'll turn it on and check the temperature before you manoeuvre Lizzie in,' James told Harriet.

Lizzie baa-ed and looked in James's direction. 'That's it, Lizzie,' he encouraged. 'Keep facing this way. Can you hear the water, girl? Nice warm water,' he added. 'Come on, then. Come and join me.'

Harriet gave Lizzie a gentle push, James reached out and took one of her horns and, talking quietly to her all the time, guided her under the spray.

'There,' he chuckled after a while. 'We're both squeaky clean now.' He led Lizzie out and the others leaped back as the Jacob shook herself.

James gave himself a quick rub with the towel before passing it to Harriet. 'I'll be back in a few minutes,' he told them as he put his T-shirt and trainers back on. 'I'll meet you in the competition tent.'

'She doesn't look as good as she did when she got here,' sighed Harriet when she'd finished rubbing Lizzie dry. 'But she'll have to do.'

Some time later, Mandy, James, and their two new friends watched hopefully as one of the judges asked Harriet to turn Lizzie first one way, then the other.

Beth slipped her hand into Mandy's and squeezed it hard. Mandy glanced down and noticed the silver signet ring on Beth's finger. Beth's mum saw Mandy looking at it and whispered, 'Now you know why we wanted to come to Animal Ark. We wanted to thank your mother for handing in Beth's ring at the police station.'

'It's Lizzie you should thank,' Mandy replied with a smile. 'The ring was lodged in a lump of dried soil that came out of her hoof.'

'Shh!' said James. 'They're getting ready to announce the winner.'

Lizzie wasn't chosen to be the sheep on the front of the calendar, but she *was* chosen to be 'Sheep of the Month' for August.

Mandy was dancing with delight when someone

tapped her on the shoulder. 'You can tell your friends that I still intend to sue,' Sam Western rasped out. 'I'll have the whole of the gliding club committee behind me. We'll find a solicitor to take the case.'

'We won't tell Harriet yet, James!' Mandy said urgently when Sam Western had moved off. 'We can't spoil this for her!'

The sheep were starting to be led out of the tent by their owners. Mandy turned to Elizabeth and thanked her for all her help. 'We'll have to go to Harriet and Lizzie now,' she said, 'and try to make sure they don't go anywhere near Mr Western.'

'We'll come with you,' said Elizabeth. 'There's something I want to tell you.'

As they all walked to where Dora had parked her trailer, Elizabeth explained that she and her husband had a reward for the finder of Beth's ring. 'Beth was heartbroken when she lost it while she was flying her kite on the moors last month,' she said. 'The ring was the last present her grandma gave her before she died. It means a lot to Beth. From what you said, Mandy, it should be Lizzie or Lizzie's owner who gets the reward.'

Harriet smiled. 'I'm glad Beth got her ring back,' she said. 'But Lizzie and I have got all the reward we want today, haven't we, August Sheep?'

Mandy and James tried hard not to show how worried they were. They met up with Dora who was standing by her trailer and actually smiling. 'Millie came first in both classes,' she said.

'And Lizzie's photo will be on the calendar page for August!' Harried laughed.

Mandy turned away, feeling troubled. Lizzie might not be here next August if Sam Western carried out his threat!

'Mandy? Why are you looking so sad?' Beth piped loudly. 'Have you lost something, like when I lost my ring?'

Mandy shook her head. 'I haven't lost anything, Beth,' she said.

'That's all right then. Oh, look. I can see my daddy. Come and meet him, Mandy. And you, James. I want to tell him about Lizzie finding my ring.'

Beth grabbed their hands and tugged them off.

'Oh!' James said, when Beth drew to a halt in front of a man both he and Mandy recognised.

Giggling and waving her hands, Beth gabbled away to her dad, telling him all about Lizzie and the ice cream and Lizzie and James in the shower. 'And . . .' she ended up, 'Guess what, Daddy? It was really the sheep who found my ring! It was inside her hoof!'

'Is that right?' Beth's father asked Mandy and James.

Mandy and James glanced quickly at each other. It was time for some quick thinking!

Mandy nodded. 'Hello again, Mr Ingrams,' she said. 'Beth told us that you're offering a reward to whoever found her ring?'

'What can we give Lizzie, Daddy?' asked Beth.

Mr Ingrams shook his head. 'We'll think of something,' he said.

'All we want is for Harriet to be allowed to keep Lizzie,' said Mandy. 'But Mr Western says he and the gliding club are going to sue Harriet's parents . . .'

'And that would mean they'd have to get rid of Lizzie!' said James.

'We don't think she'll escape again,' said Mandy, and she quickly explained how Lizzie had been getting out and how Mr Ruck was making another cattle grid.

'Now just hold on, you two!' Josh Ingrams said loudly. 'I've had just about enough of Mr Western involving me in his fight for power. Yes, that sheep has been a nuisance, but I had no part in his threat to shoot her. And I'll have no part in trying to sue her owners, either. Nor will the rest of the gliding club.

'In fact,' he went on, 'since we found out she's blind, we've all become rather fond of the pretty creature and the way she leads the other sheep into mischief. She's a gutsy character. And seeing as she found Beth's ring, she *will* have a reward. Where is she now?'

'Over by the trailers,' said James, shoving his glasses further up on to the bridge of his nose.

'Right. Bring her to the refreshment tent in ten minutes!' he ordered. Then he turned on his heels and marched off.

'But why?' asked Harriet as she led Lizzie towards the big white tent. 'Why does Beth's dad want Lizzie to go there? Is it because she found Beth's ring? I've already said we don't want a reward.'

'Don't say that until you've heard what it is,' said Dora Janeki. She'd put her sheep into the trailer and hurried after them.

'Oh, no!' Harriet said when she was close enough to make out some of the people standing by the tent. 'I can't take Lizzie there. That Mr Ingrams from the gliding club is there. Look, standing with three other men right by the way in.'

'That Mr Ingrams from the gliding club is my husband,' Elizabeth told Harriet.

Harriet gasped in horror. 'I didn't mean . . . I wasn't really being rude . . . at least, I was . . . but . . . Oh, heck,' she said, 'I wish I understood what was going on.'

'I'll tell you what's going on!' Mr Western's voice came from behind them once again. 'Mr Ingrams and some of his committee members are waiting there to inform you officially that your sheep's days are numbered.'

'That's not true, Harriet!' Elizabeth Ingrams said. 'I don't know what Josh is up to but it most certainly isn't that.'

Mandy glanced at James, then nodded meaningfully towards Lizzie and Harriet. James nodded back and between them they took hold of Harriet's arms and Lizzie's horns and hustled them over to Mr Ingrams.

Beth followed them, giggling. Dora Janeki and Elizabeth Ingrams followed more sedately.

'Mr Western is still making threats!' Mandy gasped when they got there.

'Idle, empty threats. Don't worry about them. He'll soon back down when he realises we're in complete disagreement with him. We pay a very hefty rent for the use of his field. He wouldn't like to lose that income. And now, that's enough of him. Ready, chaps?'

His companions smiled and nodded and one of them held up two bottles of lemonade. 'Should be champagne really,' he said. 'But this will have to do.'

'It's to celebrate the gliding club finally managing to find a mascot,' Mr Ingrams told them. 'That's if you agree to it, of course,' he said, looking at Harriet.

'But I don't understand,' Harriet stuttered. 'I don't know what's going on at all.'

'That's the trouble with newcomers,' said Dora Janeki. 'They can be slow to understand our ways. What the man means, Harriet, is that he wants your darned Jacob to be the club's mascot.'

'Which means you'll have to bring her up to the club on special days,' said Mr Ingrams. 'But I think Lizzie would like that, anyway.'

Baa-aaa! agreed Lizzie, moving suddenly and banging into the lemonade bottles Mr Ingrams' colleague had just opened.

'It looks like champagne anyway,' laughed Mandy

as the lemonade fizzed out all over Lizzie's face.

As Lizzie licked at the lemonade, a camera clicked and a man standing next to Mandy took out a reporter's notebook and scribbled something down. 'What a headline for the next issue,' he said. ' "Sheep at the Show Enjoying a Double Celebration".'

'It was a triple celebration for the Rucks really,' Mandy told her parents later that evening. 'Harriet's mum said there were so many people wanting to knit for her, they'd have to think about getting some more sheep!'

But, thought Mandy, as she made her way up to bed, *there'll never be another sheep like Lizzie!*

ANIMAL ARK

Lucy Daniels

1	KITTENS IN THE KITCHEN	£3.50	❐
2	PONY IN THE PORCH	£3.50	❐
3	PUPPIES IN THE PANTRY	£3.50	❐
4	GOAT IN THE GARDEN	£3.50	❐
5	HEDGEHOGS IN THE HALL	£3.50	❐
6	BADGER IN THE BASEMENT	£3.50	❐
7	CUB IN THE CUPBOARD	£3.50	❐
8	PIGLET IN A PLAYPEN	£3.50	❐
9	OWL IN THE OFFICE	£3.50	❐
10	LAMB IN THE LAUNDRY	£3.50	❐
11	BUNNIES IN THE BATHROOM	£3.50	❐
12	DONKEY ON THE DOORSTEP	£3.50	❐
13	HAMSTER IN A HAMPER	£3.50	❐
14	GOOSE ON THE LOOSE	£3.50	❐
15	CALF IN THE COTTAGE	£3.50	❐
16	KOALA IN A CRISIS	£3.50	❐
17	WOMBAT IN THE WILD	£3.50	❐
18	ROO ON THE ROCK	£3.50	❐
19	SQUIRRELS IN THE SCHOOL	£3.50	❐
20	GUINEA-PIG IN THE GARAGE	£3.50	❐
21	FAWN IN THE FOREST	£3.50	❐
22	SHETLAND IN THE SHED	£3.50	❐
23	SWAN IN THE SWIM	£3.50	❐
24	LION BY THE LAKE	£3.50	❐
25	ELEPHANTS IN THE EAST	£3.50	❐
26	MONKEYS ON THE MOUNTAIN	£3.50	❐
27	DOG AT THE DOOR	£3.50	❐
28	FOALS IN THE FIELD	£3.50	❐
29	SHEEP AT THE SHOW	£3.50	❐
	SHEEPDOG IN THE SNOW	£3.50	❐
	KITTEN IN THE COLD	£3.50	❐
	FOX IN THE FROST	£3.50	❐
	SEAL ON THE SHORE	£3.50	❐

ANIMAL ACTION

If you like Animal Ark then you'll love the RSPCA's Animal Action Club! Anyone aged 13 or under can become a member for just £5.50 a year. Join up and you can look forward to six issues of Animal Action magazine – each one is bursting with animal news, competitions, features, posters and celebrity interviews. Plus we'll send you a special membership card, badge and stickers. There are all sorts of fun things to do as well!

To be really animal-friendly just complete the form – a photocopy is fine – and send it, with a cheque or postal order for £5.50 made  payable to the RSPCA, to Animal Action Club, RSPCA, Causeway, Horsham, West Sussex RH12 1HG. We'll send you a membership pack and your first copy of *Animal Action*.

Registered charity no 219099

Don't delay, join today!

Name ....

Address ....

....

.... **Postcode** ....

Date of Birth ....

Youth membership of the Royal Society for the Prevention of Cruelty to Animals

AACHOD